The Sword Polisher's Record

The Way of Kung-Fu

The Sword Polisher's Record

The Way of Kung-Fu

Adam Hsu

CHARLES E. TUTTLE CO., INC.
Boston • Rutland, Vermont • Tokyo

First published in 1998 by Tuttle Publishing, an imprint of
Periplus Editions (HK) Ltd., with editorial offices at
153 Milk Street, Boston, Massachusetts 02109.

Library of Congress Cataloging-in-Publication Data

Hsu, Adam, 1941—
    The sword polisher's record : the way of kung-fu / Adam Hsu.—
1st ed.
      p. cm.
    ISBN 0-8048-3138-6 (pbk.)
     1. Kung-fu. 2. Kung-fu—Health aspects. I. Title.
    GV1114.7.H78 1998
    796.815'9—dc21   97-45549
                                          CIP

Distributed by

USA	Japan	Southeast Asia
Tuttle Publishing	Tuttle Shokai Ltd.	Berkeley Books Pte. Ltd.
RR 1 Box 231-5	1-21-13, Seki	5 Little Road #08-01
North Clarendon, VT	Tama-ku, Kawasaki-shi 214	Singapore 536983
05759	Japan	Tel.: (65) 280-3320
Tel.: (802) 773-8930	Tel.: (044) 833-0225	Fax: (65) 280-6290
Fax: (802) 773-6993	Fax: (044) 822-0413	

First edition

05 04 03 02 01 01 00 99 98 1 3 5 7 9 10 8 6 4 2

Printed in Singapore

Acknowledgments

This book could not have been published without the help of several of my students including Dan Farber, Richard Miller, Hal Malmud, and Marie Anthony. They contributed to the writing and editing of this book. I also want to thank Marie Anthony for many for the photographs included in this book. In addition, Meilin Wong assisted in preparing the manuscript for publication, and Ken Watanabe contributed illustrations.

Table Of Contents

Preface ix

Part 1: Knocking on the Kung-fu Door 11
The Contemporary Purpose of Kung-fu 12
Traditional Kung-fu: The Complete Exercise 16
The Simple Fact of Yin and Yang 20

Part 2: The Foundation of Kung-fu 25
Mapping Kung-fu's DNA 26
Drafting a Kung-fu Constitution 33
Stance Training 42
Kung-fu's Way to Power 46
How Much Flexibility is Enough for Kung-fu? 50

Part 3: Myth and Reality of Kung-fu Styles 53
The Real Difference Between Internal
 and External Kung-fu 54
The Myth of Shaolin Kung-fu 59
The Internal Dilemma 66
The Dividing Line Between Northern
 and Southern Styles 68
Should the Many Be One? 72
A Lifelong Commitment to One Style 76
Piecing Together the Kung-fu Puzzle 80
Counterfeit Kung-fu 84

Part 4: The Role of Forms in Kung-fu 89
Is It Necessary to Learn Forms? 90
Form Without Content 94
Analyze Your Beauty 98
Forms and Function 102
Two-Person Forms: Martial or Performing Art? 106

Part 5: Mind and Body Training   109
Starting with a Clean Slate   110
"Don't Tickle My Stomach"   113
Learning to See   116
Find Your Balance   120
Internal Training: Is It Necessary?   123
Kung-fu Mind, Multi-dimensional Mind   128
The Risk of Special Training   133
Adapting Western Methods to Kung-fu   136

Part 6: Usage: The Soul of Kung-fu   141
The Kung-fu Art of Fighting   142
Real Kung-fu: Use It or Lose It!   147
Use Your Head, Not Your Opponent's   153
The Continuous Fist   156
The Nine Doors of Kung-fu   159

Part 7: Masters and Students   165
How to Choose a Kung-fu Teacher   166
Only a Kung-fu Teacher   171
The Proper Kung-fu Attitude   175
Kung-fu's Age of Reason   178
The Senior Student   183
Belt Levels for Kung-fu   186
Salute! I'm Your Grandpa   189

Part 8: Kung-fu Today and Tomorrow   193
The Complete Kung-fu Practitioner   194
The True Lessons of Fighting   197
Pursuing the Ultimate Kung-fu Goals   200

About the Author   205

Preface

When I arrived in San Francisco from Taiwan in 1978, my dream was to help promote and preserve the ancient arts that had been handed down by my forebears. I have studied kung-fu since I was a young boy, learning from my father and then from the best teachers I could find in Taiwan. I feel fortunate to have been exposed to the ancient treasures of kung-fu, and view it as my duty to share those treasures with others in the United States and elsewhere.

In 1980, I went Los Angeles to discuss writing articles for *Black Belt* magazine with Jim Nail, who was editor of the publication at that time. He approached me about writing a monthly column for the martial arts magazine. When I returned to San Francisco, I felt unclear as to what direction to take with the column. Words and theory are not a substitute for the physical and mental training required to polish one's kung-fu. Yet, they are an essential part of the learning process, allowing the mind to process commands and concepts that help the body move in a special, kung-fu way.

The meaning of words, however, can be bent and distorted to have a detrimental effect on kung-fu. In fact, today kung-fu is like a sword of incomparable value that has lost its shine and sharpness—a result of the many misconceptions spawned from the words and images in books, movies, TV shows, and video games.

The errant teachings of unqualified instructors have also greatly contributed to the uncertainty of kung-fu's future. Students desiring the real kung-fu are unwittingly cheated by instructors promoting fraudulent histories, self-made family trees, and so-called "secret" teachings.

In addition, mainland China's government-produced wushu (martial art) has jeopardized the future of traditional kung-fu. The movements in the popular wushu forms promoted throughout the world contradict almost all the fundamentals of kung-fu.

Based on kung-fu becoming an endangered discipline, it became obvious to me that the column needed to help restore kung-fu's definition, purity, principles, and basic theory. "The Sword Polisher's Record," as I named the column, became my way to polish the kung-fu sword, clearing up the misconceptions that are causing it to become dull and rusty.

This book includes many of the original "The Sword Polisher's Record" columns printed in *Black Belt* and *Wu Shu Kung-fu* magazines. Additional articles that first appeared in *Inside Kung-fu* magazine are also included to provide more depth on some of the topics.

The book is organized into eight interconnected sections, each examining a different aspect of kung-fu. The first sections deal with the foundations of kung-fu. Without developing a true foundation, no matter the style, there is no kung-fu. In subsequent sections, I try to bring to light important concepts and principles related to kung-fu styles and forms, as well as usage and training. Finally, I discuss the future of kung-fu and its place in our lives.

I hope you find *The Sword Polisher's Record* useful. My dream will be fulfilled if we can restore this damaged treasure so that its beauty and power can enrich us today and in the generations to come.

—*Adam Hsu*
October, 1997

Part 1

Knocking on the Kung-fu Door

The Contemporary Purpose of Kung-fu

Before the introduction and dominance of guns in warfare, skill in hand-to-hand combat determined the victor in any battle. Armies were trained in martial art. The security of communities, villages, and a person's family depended on successful martial art training.

In ancient China, the weapons available were limited to those people could wield with their hands: the staff, saber, sword, spear, and of course the primary weapon, the body. In these times the attitude and purpose of kung-fu was very serious, potentially a matter of life and death. With survival as its foremost purpose, kung-fu was learned not for its beauty or meditative qualities, but for protecting one's family and possessions.

Certainly the ancient practitioners derived considerable health benefits as a by-product of their art. Kung-fu training emphasizes use of the entire body. The body is trained to maneuver in and out of unorthodox positions with fluidity and control. The martial artists of old were not without appreciation for this valuable consequence of training, but their chief purpose for learning kung-fu was self-defense.

With the introduction of guns to warfare, the weapons of old became quickly obsolete, and the highly evolved art of kung-fu can be said to have reached its evolutionary peak. Because of the deadly power and accuracy of the gun, the role of hand-to-hand combat was greatly diminished. Naturally, with this descent of kung-fu's importance in battle, the training associated with it also lost value and intensity. Why train with devotion and sincerity if a bullet can defeat your mightiest technique?

Although hand-to-hand combat has become less a factor in warfare, the ancient art of kung-fu has endured. Today, in fact, it is enjoying a revitalization not only in China but the world over. Many people have taken notice of kung-fu and have proved by their interest and participation that it most assuredly has a place in the modern world.

Kung-fu skills, which have been refined over the centuries, are not learned easily or quickly.

Kung-fu is thousands of years old and is a highly developed system of martial art. The student who locates a good kung-fu school will find the training thorough and challenging. Kung-fu skills, which have been refined over centuries, are not learned easily or quickly. The sincere student, however, through hard work and dedication, will not be disappointed with the results.

Although people no longer need to learn kung-fu for survival, those who do study for the purpose of martial art will realize that it remains an excellent system of self-defense.

Although hand-to-hand combat has become less a factor in warfare, the ancient art of kung-fu has endured.

Today, it is common knowledge that daily exercise benefits one's health, appearance, and mental state. Kung-fu uses the whole body in a way that exercises and strengthens all the muscles, tendons, and ligaments. Unlike most Western exercise, sports, and recreational activities, which focus primarily on external training, kung-fu works on harmonizing the external and the internal.

Some training routines have been developed exclusively for their specialized health benefits. The unique coiling and uncoiling movements of kung-fu can massage the body's inner organs and lymphatic system. A particular exercise, for example, may correspond to the area and functioning of a single organ. I am of the opinion that kung-fu is unsurpassed as a system for all-around conditioning.

The mental benefits of kung-fu are not as easily measured as the physical ones. You can't just look in a mirror and see the changes and improvements kung-fu training has made on your perceptions, attitudes, and feelings, but often it is these inner changes that are the most profound.

If you are not prepared to invest years of practice, don't expect to advance far in the art.

"Kung-fu" literally means time and hard work. I can say unequivocally that there are no shortcuts. The impatient student finds only frustration. If you are not prepared to invest years of practice, then don't expect to advance far in the art. Those who make the investment, on the other hand, certainly will benefit mentally and physically. Discipline, confidence, understanding one's limitations, and belief in one's abilities are all gained from the practice of kung-fu.

Another key element that attracts people to kung-fu is its undeniable beauty. Kung-fu combines power, grace, and agility. Some kung-fu styles emphasize the dance-like and acrobatic quali-

Each morning at sunrise, hundreds of people gather in China's parks to begin the day with healthy exercise.

ties of kung-fu. For the performance-oriented student, kung-fu can be a majestic and flamboyant means of self-expression. Forms competitions can provide a platform for displaying one's abilities and a springboard for recognition.

I have tried to reveal that kung-fu has not just one purpose. We see how it can improve our health, that it can be treated as an art form and studied for its beauty, or studied for its original intent, martial art. Kung-fu can develop one's strength and flexibility, and nourish qualities such as patience, discipline, and confidence.

Like everything that lives, kung-fu is ceaselessly changing. It has proven valuable and resilient enough to endure the sweeping changes of centuries, and to arrive here in the present like an ancient treasure forever being rediscovered.

Traditional Kung-fu: the Complete Exercise

The number and variety of exercise activities available to us today is staggering. You can choose from among baseball, football, soccer, track and field, water sports, winter sports, aerobics, weight training, and cross training to name a few. Why would we ever need kung-fu as an exercise?

In my opinion, it's difficult to find any sport or activity that can top kung-fu as an overall form of exercise. For all traditional kung-fu practitioners, even those whose main purpose is self-defense, daily martial arts practice can prevent illness, create a better life, and reach for longevity. In other words, martial arts is a form of exercise that is wholesome, unique, and complete.

> Kung-fu training addresses the needs of the inside as well as the outside.

What makes kung-fu such great exercise? In reality, exercise doesn't adequately describe the overall quality of kung-fu. In Chinese, the term *yun dong* is used to define this activity. Chinese-English and English-Chinese dictionaries typically translate *yun dong* as exercise, sports, recreation, or athletics. However, these English words somehow translate only *dong*, not *yun*.

A better translation for *dong* is movement, action, and mobility. Motions like waving the arms, kicking the legs, twisting the body, and shaking the head are all visible, whether executed alone or with a team, or with a ball, a stick, or a racquet. All are *dong*.

I agree that all these types of exercise are valuable and good for the health, but *yun* is missing. In China *yun* and *dong* are never separated. *Yun* means "internal," including breath, circulation, mind control, and focus.

Generally, *dong* deals more with muscle, tendon, bone, and skeletal structure. *Yun* is more associated with the organs, nervous system, brain, and feeling. A young tennis player, for example, would usually play with lots of *dong*, relying mostly on external strength. Overdoing *dong* can potentially lead to health problems because the *yun* is neglected. Internal and external must be balanced and the exercise must be complete, if we are to really benefit ourselves and others. Good exercise should always be safe, and we should enjoy a sweet aftertaste that lasts several hours, several days, or even weeks.

Internal and external must be balanced and the exercise must be complete, if we are to really benefit ourselves and others.

When we are young, we can enjoy lots of external movement. When we get older, we become less active and can't as easily enjoy large movements, speed, high impact, and quick twisting of the muscles. Unfortunately, this is exactly the time our bodies really begin to need good exercise to maintain youthful energy and health. Most of the exercise systems available in our society can't satisfy this need.

I don't agree with so-called low impact, low-key approach where the contents of the exercise are the same but the dosage less. We need a better prescription to exercise the body inside and out. The kung-fu way is the better way.

There are approximately 250 kung-fu styles—northern, southern, external, internal, long-range, short-range—and numerous weapons. They all have something in common.

Please don't mistakenly believe mainland China's government-sanctioned wushu (lit., "martial art") is traditional Chinese kung-fu. Modern wushu has more in common with Western exercise than traditional Chinese kung-fu. From Western exercise, wushu practitioners learn to keep moving (running, jumping, and tumbling) and to discard internal training. They skip the *yun*. Some call it Chinese ballet. Can we call it Chinese aerobics? For kung-fu to be a complete exercise, it must be practiced correctly in the kung-fu way.

Our everyday common sense tells us that no movement equals no exercise, and therefore no health benefits should result. I think everyone, even those who've never done any kung-fu, can try a simple, scientific experiment. Pick one posture and hold it for awhile. I believe that before three minutes is up your body will experience the same symptoms as if you were exercising. After five minutes, your body's responses will be quite strong. I doubt that untrained people can last for a full ten minutes, even a boxer, football player, or bodybuilder. Judged by kung-fu training requirements, ten minutes is really a very short period of time.

Sifu Liu Yun Chiao, the author's teacher, holds the baquazhang bear posture.

If you have access to the equipment and resources to conduct research on this type of stationary exercise, you will see that it actually provides the same results: the pulse rate increases, respiration increases, and more oxygen is pumped into the blood. An easier way to measure the results is by our own sweat.

Moving exercise, *dong,* is somehow like an investment. An expenditure of energy is required to move the body. When we are young, we have more than enough to invest and can enjoy any returns, no matter how small. As we age, we no longer can afford to invest so freely. Our reserve is much smaller and the risk much greater.

On the other hand, *yun* exercise yields a very high return for a much smaller investment. The prime attraction of *dong* exercise is recreational. Health benefits are a side effect. *Dong* looks outward; *yun* looks inward, focusing our attention on our own body (inside and out) and spirit, thus directly providing benefits to our health. *Yun* doesn't provide any distractions to divert our attention away from the prime business at hand—rejuvenation of our body, organs, and spirit.

Yun and *dong* do not conflict. Instead, when practiced together, they are powerful partners, creating a rich yield of health, fitness, mental clarity, focus, and energy for all of us.

The Simple Fact of Yin and Yang

Almost every martial artist knows something about the Chinese theory of *yin* and *yang*. Some practitioners try to apply the principles of this theory to improve their technique. Though a useful idea, the theory of *yin* and *yang* has been overemphasized and misunderstood in the martial arts. Many people treat *yin* and *yang* like an unfathomable truth, an idea that cannot be fully grasped. This respectful attitude, however, does not help to make the concept any more accessible or useful in learning martial arts. The fact is that *yin* and *yang* are not beyond our grasp: they are an integral part of daily life and a practical way of explaining an essential aspect of existence.

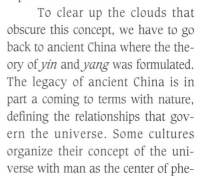

To clear up the clouds that obscure this concept, we have to go back to ancient China where the theory of *yin* and *yang* was formulated. The legacy of ancient China is in part a coming to terms with nature, defining the relationships that govern the universe. Some cultures organize their concept of the universe with man as the center of phenomena. Thus, nature is something that must be conquered and made to conform to human reason.

Chinese philosophy is based on a different perspective. The Chinese people sought to harmonize with nature rather than to dominate it. The theory of *yin* and *yang* was developed as a practical way of describing and classifying this universe in which humanity is a part of nature, rather than the master of nature. The Chinese perceive the universe as the interaction of complementary opposites such as day and night, male

Yin and yang represent the continual process of change and flux in nature.

and female, hard and soft, life and death: *yang* and *yin*. The dynamic cycle of creation and destruction (embodied in the life cycle of a flower, for example) is seen as a continuous process of change.

Perhaps the best way to understand this theory is to visualize the geometric representation of *yin* and *yang* (see Fig. 1). Western culture, unlike Chinese culture, classifies phenomena into fixed opposites; for example, day and night could be configured as a square divided in half.

This relationship could also be depicted within a circular shape that shows how the opposites together form a whole. Neither of these conceptions show any interaction between the opposites, a typically Western perspective. In Chinese culture, however, *yin* and *yang* are configured within a circular shape that expresses the interaction and complementary nature of opposites.

The curving line that connects the two entities expresses change, the basic idea underlying the theory of *yin* and *yang*. *Yin* and *yang*, therefore, represent the continual process of change and flux in nature: day *(yang)* is always changing into night *(yin)* and night is always changing into day. This relationship is most fully illustrated by the taiji diagram.

Not only do *yin* and *yang* continuously interact, but the *yin* always contains some *yang*, and the *yang* always contains some *yin*. No pure *yin* or *yang* exists, only varying degrees of inter-

Figure 1

action between the two. The essence of this idea is found in the Chinese saying: "Creation never stops: *yang* reaches its limit and gives birth to *yin; yin* reaches its limit and gives birth to *yang*."

The Chinese use the theory of *yin* and *yang* to explain all facets of life, such as medicine, painting, architecture, weather, food, and kung-fu. Comprehending this theory is not essential to the practice of kung-fu or any other art. Many of the old masters were illiterate and could not explain their art, but their kung-fu naturally conformed to the principles of *yin* and

> *Many of the old masters were illiterate and could not explain their art, but their kung-fu naturally conformed to the principles of yin and yang.*

yang. Mastering kung-fu is impossible without knowingly or unknowingly following the principles of this theory.

Although philosophy is not a substitute for physical training, understanding *yin* and *yang* can help practitioners improve their technique. Western culture, for example, evolved based on a philosophical foundation that typically views concepts as fixed, or black and white. Grasping the theory of *yin* and *yang* serves to bridge that cultural gap and demonstrate a fundamental aspect of kung-fu.

The theory of *yin* and *yang* as applied to the martial arts is quite practical. In a settled stance, for example, all the parts of the body in shadow are considered *yin,* and the remaining parts, *yang.* In the taijiquan movement *danbian* (single whip), the shaded areas and the backside of the body are *yin* (Fig. 2). Since kung-fu is not a static form, *yin* and *yang* can also be applied to the body in motion. In general, any outward movement is considered *yang* and any inward movement is *yin. Danbian* is basically a *yang* movement: both arms and the leg clearly extend outward. When considering this movement from beginning to end, rather than the climax of the movement, or taijiquan (or any kung-fu style) in general, the *yin* and *yang* constantly change.

At the beginning of the movement both the arms and legs are closer to the body *(yin)* (Fig. 3). Then the leg moves out and the whole body uncoils in a highly coordinated twisting action to complete the movement. Note how the arm changes from *yin,* facing the body to *yang,* facing and extended away from the body.

Other aspects that characterize a movement are also classified as *yin* or *yang.* Any movement that is hard, fast, strong, or clear is *yang;* movements that are softer, slower, or less obvious are *yin.* Then *jing* (power) that is stored or released is also described similarly in terms of *yin* and *yang.* In a major attacking movement *(yang),* for instance, there are smaller, supporting movements that are *yin.* In *danbian* the shoulder, hip, and knee are less obvious parts of the body that may be used in attacking. Kung-fu never violates the principles of *yin* and *yang*—the *yang* always contains some *yin* and the *yin* contains some *yang.* As the saying goes: "*Yin* by itself cannot create; *yang* by itself cannot grow."

> *When the power and movements are balanced and calm, not committed to any fixed pattern, then the percentage of yin and yang jing used to issue the power can easily be changed as the situation demands.*

In the taiji diagram *yin* and *yang* are mixed, with some *yin* in the *yang* and vice versa. In terms of *jing,* the soft *(yin)* and hard *(yang)* energies are mixed in the same way. Soft and hard does not mean weak and strong; it simply implies different kinds of power. Having the ability to manage the *jing* is important in kung-fu. For example, being able to balance the *yin* and *yang jing* has many advantages. Because you don't know which part of your body you will have to use to attack or defend, or the expertise of your opponent, a calm, balanced awareness should be maintained. When the power and movements are balanced and calm, not committed to any fixed pattern, then the percentage of *yin* and *yang jing* used to issue the power can easily be changed as the situation demands.

Figure 2

Figure 3

The training of baguazhang emphasizes this idea. Another name for baguazhang—*yin yang bapanzhang* (*yin* and *yang* eight circling palm)—aptly describes this system. *Yin* and *yang* are continually changing in the circular twisting movements, but the *jing* is balanced. Of course, the percentage of *yin* and *yang* changes when a weakness is created or appears in the opponent's defense, and the power is issued.

The art of xingyiquan has three levels of training for power. *Ming jing* (clear) develops the obvious, more observable energy. *An jing* (dark) develops the concealed, less obvious energy, and *hua jing* (melting) combines the clear *(yang)* and dark *(yin)* as in the taiji diagram. At the higher levels of any kung-fu system, the practitioner is able to control the *jing,* and direct the flow of energy as well as the movement of the body according to the principles of *yin* and *yang.*

Understanding the theory of *yin* and *yang* can give insight into the depth and sophistication of Chinese philosophy and kung-fu. Both kung-fu and the theory of *yin* and *yang* were developed to satisfy the practical needs of the ancient Chinese. Acquiring that understanding is best accomplished through practical, direct experience such as learning kung-fu. Then the theory becomes a reality.

Part 2

The Foundation
of Kung-fu

Mapping Kung-fu's DNA

We definitely live in a modern age compared to the world in which kung-fu originated. Every day more science fiction becomes science fact as a rapidly increasing array of technological wonders enhance our daily lives. Nowadays when we have a problem or mystery to solve, we can choose from many sophisticated tools to help clear away the confusion and lead us to the truth. DNA testing, for instance, is used in such diverse areas as archaeology, criminology, and medicine. These high-tech tools not only provide society with sophisticated, reliable investigative techniques but also affect our individual attitudes. Today, we are more prone to gather convincing evidence before jumping to conclusions.

This kind of scientific examination should also be applied to the study of kung-fu. You can avoid shedding tears and sweating blood in an all-out journey to a martial arts dead end by discovering the kung-fu DNA, the building blocks that make up authentic kung-fu. Following are some of the core kung-fu building blocks derived from my investigations and experience. The list is by no means complete, and only a beginning attempt to map out a complete DNA of traditional kung-fu.

Stance training builds a very strong foundation, which is absolutely essential to perform kung-fu's whole-body usage techniques.

Horse stance

Although the horse stance is used in many non-Chinese systems, kung-fu's needs are different from other martial arts. Stance training builds a very strong foundation, which is absolutely essential to perform kung-fu's whole-body usage techniques. In the kung-fu horse stance, the practitioner's toes must point straight ahead, feet parallel, and knees angled slightly inward. While it is incorrect to point the knees out, the thighs must stay open creating a rounded, not sharp, angle at the groin. The buttocks should not protrude or be lower than the knees.

All empty-leg stances are potential kicks, knee strikes, and sweeps.

Empty-leg stance

With the empty-leg stance, all weight is on the supporting leg, and none on the front leg. All empty-leg stances are potential kicks, knee strikes, and leg sweeps. The empty leg may also be called upon to move forward, backward, to the side, or into a twisting step at an instant without the body first having to shift its weight distribution. In kung-fu's empty stance, the front leg must be fully available for these uses.

Kicks do not use the arms for balance

During a kick, the arms are either performing other techniques or in a ready position, prepared to initiate an appropriate response to the opponent's movements. In kung-fu, the relationship between legs and arms is that of equal partners in attack and defense, not subordinates to a principle worker. Using the arms to balance the body during kicks is a natural tendency, but in terms of kung-fu usage it is untrained and immature technique.

The entire body finishes moving at the same time

There are two common ways the timing of movements lacks full coordination. Part of the body finishes its movement while other parts are still traveling to completion, or the lower body settles into a stance and remains inert while the upper body follows with several attack and defense techniques. In kung-fu, the entire body, not just the arms, must work as one unit. Power issuing depends on unbroken, coordinated movement throughout the entire body. In addition, every part of the body must keep moving at all times to sustain the momentum of a usage technique.

Punch from the spine

Punches must originate from the spine, not the shoulders. The kung-fu practitioner's two arms become a single coordinated unit, beginning with the fingers of one hand, traveling up the arm, through the shoulders, across the upper back, and down to the fingertips of the second hand. When one arm extends, the other one compliments the movement like parts of a pulley system.

Both fists hit the same target

As the first fist withdraws after punching to make way for an attack from the other fist, the second hits exactly the same spot, replacing the first. Opponents always try to open up leaks and penetrate a practitioner's guard. Punches that hit the target side-by-side give the opponent an open channel to invade into the practitioner's space.

Split attention

The kung-fu practitioner must be able to manage different areas of the body simultaneously rather than focusing on a single area or body part. Awareness must extend beyond arms and legs to include the entire body. In addition, because our attention quite naturally tends to fixate on what we can see or what we have targeted (such as an opponent), we must train ourselves to pay attention to what is around us at all times. For example, kung-fu training requires positioning an arm behind the body in a specific position. A fist extended out behind the shoulder must stay

> *The kung-fu practitioner must be able to manage different areas of the body simultaneously, rather than focusing on a single area or body part.*

at ear level, and a hooked hand must be held out behind the back at a 45-degree angle. This training isn't easy, but if you can manage the space behind, then other directions and angles are also better controlled.

Joints are never locked

Locking the joints, such as the elbows or knees, is damaging to both physical health and martial art. From a health standpoint, joint locking can lead to stiffness and strains as well as more serious injuries. From the standpoint of usage, a locked joint pushes movements to their dead end, killing any potential for last minute changes in the movement. As a result, the rhythm and fluency within a sequence of movements is destroyed.

The joints must never be locked.

Never hyperextend the shoulders and back

In kung-fu, the shoulders should be in line with the chest, never pulled to the rear with the back arched and chest pushed out. Any martial art requires the practitioner to have an on-guard for protection. The arms should function as double doors, remaining closed to guard the chest. Over-stretched shoulders force the gate open, causing unnecessary and meaningless exposure to attack. Exaggerated and boldly stated postures also violate Chinese aesthetics, which finds beauty in restraint.

Breath through the nose

Except for yells, the mouth should stay shut. Keep the teeth together and touch the tongue to the roof of the mouth, placed behind the front teeth. Since taking air through the mouth usually results in short breaths, an open mouth encourages shallow breathing into the chest, panting, and gasping for air. Basic kung-fu breathing exercises train the practitioner to inhale and exhale long, deep breaths through the nose because this prevents or at least delays the onset of gasping and hyperventilation. Practically speaking, the practitioner can last longer without running out of oxygen.

Qi is held in the dantian

The most obvious and common error is holding *qi* (energy circulating in the body) in the upper torso, forcing the chest to become tense and the shoulders to elevate too high. In the upper levels of traditional kung-fu, even when the practitioner sends the *qi* to other areas of the body, the *dantian* (place in the lower abdomen) is never totally emptied. Any of China's traditional body disciplines— health exercises, neigong, Beijing opera, folk dance, acrobatics, kung-fu—always require the *qi* to sink, never rise up and center in the chest because to do so will encourage short, shallow breathing and ultimately damage health.

> *Training is by nature primarily external as the student learns the basics; internal elements are layered into the training as the student progresses to higher levels.*

Internal and external must go together

All kung-fu styles require both internal and external training if the practitioner is to reach the higher levels. One without the other is incomplete. This is true whether the styles are labeled hard, soft, external, or internal. At the outset, training is by nature primarily external as the student learns the basics; internal aspects of training are layered into the training as the student progresses to higher levels.

No preparatory motions

Techniques must be executed without special set up, such as running to build momentum for a leap or extra steps to help the delivery of a tornado kick. Every extra movement or preparation takes time, and a split second could mean the difference between success and failure in a fighting situation. To take advantage of a leak in an opponent's guard, the practitioner must be able to attack from wherever the arm is positioned without preparatory motions. For example, drawing back the arm after a punch to gain distance for a second technique violates the kung-fu principles. The correct method involves the entire torso, using a powerful twist at the spine to send out the shoulder, elbow, and palm or fist to deliver the second blow. Forms that include running sequences to boost the practitioner's leaps are more performance art and don't enhance real kung-fu training.

All movements contain chan si jin

There are no straight movements in kung-fu. Movements are curved and involve twisting action, following the principle of *chan si jin* (silk reeling energy). Even during what appears to be a straight punch, the fist and arm quickly rotate, drilling toward the target. Blocks do not slam directly against the opponent's arm but twist as they make contact to reduce the speed and power of the attack, redirecting the force away from the practitioner, and possibly creating a leak for retaliation.

Global awareness

The kung-fu practitioner must be aware of the surrounding space, never standing at the edge but in the middle of a globe ready to exert energy or force in any direction. This broader awareness runs contrary to our normal mode of perception. The mind is usually filled with a tangle of extraneous thoughts as

The kung-fu practitioner must be aware of the surrounding space, never standing at the edge but in the middle of a globe ready to exert energy or force in any direction.

we go about our daily lives. However, kung-fu is incomplete unless it trains the mind, enlarging the practitioner's mental capacity to include the space around him. When this global awareness is present, it can be seen very clearly in the postures.

Multipurpose movement

Each movement in kung-fu, whether defense or attack, always has more than one purpose. Therefore, the meaning of movements is not completely clear in the beginning, and they are rich in possibilities until the target is reached. Defensive and offensive techniques are interchangeable. An attacking punch can also be a blocking move, and the practitioner should be able to change the direction and focus of a movement as the situation demands. Single-point techniques delivered and then pulled back to redeliver do not follow kung-fu principles.

Double-layered training

Kung-fu training exercises, forms, and movements should not be designed and practiced with the sole intention of destroying an opponent. Real kung-fu training must enrich the entire human being, improving health, developing physical and mental abilities, and expanding one's philosophical outlook and worldview. This is why kung-fu is such an outstanding and beneficial discipline for our society. The martial artist who tries to transform his human body into a human robot or super fighting machine is making a big mistake and demeaning the art of kung-fu. Practitioners should always check to make sure that their training is really kung-fu—educating and enhancing the body, mind, and spirit.

When you search for a good kung-fu coach, use this kung-fu DNA checklist. These principles can help you evaluate the authenticity of their kung-fu training, and you won't be swayed by beautiful costumes, flashy movements, mesmerizing background music, self-made family trees, or movements that contradict the way of traditional kung-fu.

Drafting a Kung-fu Constitution

Kung-fu styles share a common foundation. Historically, kung-fu was born of the struggle for survival and was refined over centuries of accumulated experience and wisdom as Chinese medicine, health exercise, and martial arts evolved. The common foundation can be codified into basic principles that apply to most kung-fu styles. Without them, even the most graceful, flowing, beautiful performance is simply fake kung-fu. Just as in the realm of living things a fox is not a bird, such a form could not truthfully be categorized as kung-fu.

These principles are the most basic starting point, rather than the highest level requirements. Students who are willing to start at the fundamental levels will progress in the correct direction. After all, the tallest peak can only be conquered by starting at the very base of the mountain, and then climbing diligently, step by step, to the higher plateaus. The key is to begin at the beginning; high level short cuts can only lead to dead ends.

The key is to begin at the beginning; high level short cuts can only lead to dead ends.

Each of these basic principles relates to the body, and how it must be used within kung-fu movements.

Head

The head must be held straight, and the neck relaxed. Do not allow an intense focus and serious attitude to tighten your neck or unconsciously push your head forward. Imagine an object resting on top of your head that must not fall off. It should be light like a piece of paper, leaf, or feather—small but always present. It should feel as if something in the sky were slowly pulling up on your hair,

gently but firmly helping to keep your head straight. Every hair is pulled, from the back of the neck to the top of the skull. The overall feeling is somewhat like a puppet, whose head is being lifted by strings manipulated from above.

The head must be held straight, and the neck relaxed.

Eyes

The eyelids should be normal and relaxed. The eyes should not be tense or bugged out. The gaze should not be lowered, even while you focus inward to get the feeling of sinking the *qi*. The mind, not the eyes, is responsible for maintaining inner awareness and feeling. The eyes should be set like middle C, the center of the piano keyboard. The eyes follow the movement, turning left, right, up, or down, but only in conjunction with the head as it turns.

Nose

The breath flows only through the nostrils, not the mouth. Breathing should be slow, even, gentle—the less noticeable, the

Breathing should be slow, even, gentle—the less noticeable, the better.

better. However, you should feel an inner physical sensation of expansion throughout the face and internal passageways—from the nostrils, up the nose, into the entire face, and extending down into the chin and throat. This feeling of expansion should continue throughout the inhalation and exhalation.

Mouth

The lips should always stay closed but without tension. The teeth should always maintain contact but without tension. The tongue should touch the roof of the mouth just behind the front teeth and stay there at all times. Let the saliva accumulate until it has to be swallowed. Never spit it out. Swallow slowly, or ingest the saliva with several small swallows.

Shoulders

You must learn to sink the shoulders. They must be carried without tension, rather than pulled high in the manner of a soldier at attention. The first step is to achieve relaxation within the mind. Then place attention on preventing the shoulders from rising. After these steps are accomplished, you can begin to generate a sinking feeling in the shoulders. Do not try to fabricate the feeling by angling the spine, bending the shoulders forward, and sticking the neck out.

Back

Kung-fu requires *ba bei*. *Ba* means to yank or pull but it also means stretch and straighten up. *Bei* means the back. The entire spine—including the areas behind and in front of it—must be held straight. A straight spine is equivalent to a clean, white piece of paper totally available to receive writing or drawing. A common misinterpretation of the *ba bei* rule is to extend the spine upward while bending, head stretched out, and chest caved in. Under these circumstances, no matter how hard you try, any words you write will be unreadable because they have filled the clean, white sheet of paper with scribbles.

Ba can also be interpreted as alert. *Tin ba* means to straighten up physically. *Jin ba* means to remain alert and sensitive to inner feelings. The implication is that during any movement, the spinal column must be straightened both in front and back. This concept is fundamental and incontrovertible. Any movement or posture that contradicts this principle, contradicts the entire constitution.

Chest

One of kung-fu's rules is *han xiong*. *Han* means containing something or capacity; *xiong* means chest. *Han* can also be interpreted as "swallow" or "inward" in the Chinese language, and thus many practitioners misinterpret the term to mean bending the spine. This posture is another violation of the kung-fu constitution and may cause damage to the lungs.

In fact, *han xiong* does not mean to stick out the chest and hyperextend the back, a posture required by many Western body disciplines. This raises the *qi* too high, and brings tension into the chest and related areas including the stomach and shoulders. Basically, you should stay relaxed and refrain from pushing out your chest.

Later in the training, *han xiong* will lead to a deeper interpretation. *Han xiong* also means empty space, like the inside of an envelope or box. Because the chest is at the front of the body, quite naturally it gets lots of attention, and movement, in daily life. However, kung-fu asks you to keep the chest empty. Let the back lead and the chest follow.

Stomach

You should start with an calm stomach. Don't use power, and don't tighten up. Keep the stomach soft like a suede leather bag. During movements, the stomach should not be self-motivated or independent but, just like the chest, be led by the back and waist. This will make it possible to send *qi* down to the center of the abdominal area, the *dantian.*

Only after enough *qi* has accumulated in the *dantian*—like money in a bank—will practitioners feel solidity, strength, heat, desire, or will in the *dantian.* That feeling must come from the inside out. At the same time, the stomach should remain relaxed.

An awareness should now be developing that the back is controlling the *chan si jin* twisting movements. The waist, which is in charge of horizontal twisting *chan si jin* movement, cooperates with the back. First, the waist must stay totally relaxed so it can be available for any movement. Second, it must stay level, not tipped over or off balance.

The waist could be called the joint that links the upper with the lower body. If it moves incorrectly, then the human body will be split into two pieces and lose its integrity. Incorrect practice will totally destroy all of one's good intentions and efforts.

The palms should not be stretched out but held in a naturally open, relaxed manner

Hips

The hips provide the major support for the waist. They must be relaxed and balanced. Normally they don't have a large degree of motion. However, quite often they are the leaders or vanguard of the waist's movement. The hips are very important for shrinking and expanding the body. Sometimes merely shifting the hips without taking any steps can change your body's position.

Buttocks

The buttocks must follow the spine's direction from the very top down to the tip of the tail bone, maintaining a 90-degree angle to the ground. The buttocks should not stick out, but at the same time it should not be overemphasized by tucking under or intentionally pushing the hips forward. Incorrect positioning creates tension and bothers the tail bone, tipping it forward, off-center from the plane of the spine. Correct positioning for the buttocks is smooth, straight, and 90-degrees to the ground.

Rectum

In Chinese martial arts, the term *ming dang* means to close the inner groin and buttocks area. *Dang* is not merely a polite name for this particular body part. The term refers to the entire area, not only the rectum itself. People commonly misinterpret this to mean they should suck in and seal the anus (contract the sphincter muscle). This technique is unhealthy, interferes with movements

A heaviness or sinking should be felt throughout the entire area, including back and upper arm.

and will not enhance sexual ability. Beginners should follow the advice from the previous section: Don't stick out the buttocks, keep the spine straight. Don't pay any extra attention to the anus. Instead you should try to remain relaxed so that the ligaments, muscles, and tendons can be fully stretched out.

Later on in the training, you should *chen dang,* meaning sink down. Open up, stretch out, expand the groin area—with some intention to push the buttocks down toward the ground. This will help to stretch the legs wider and reach out with a bigger step. Eventually, the *ming dang* can be done correctly: the entire genital and rectal area elevates upward.

Elbows

In everyday life, people have a natural tendency to raise and open up their elbows. Therefore, you must pay special attention to drop the elbows and avoid opening them up or stretching them outward. Later on in the training, you should attempt to achieve the sensation of weighted elbows. They must feel as if something is pulling the skin down from under the elbows, causing them to drop. Eventually they must attain a sinking or heavy feeling, not only at the elbow but throughout the entire area including the back and upper arm. While moving or shifting posture, the heaviness will also shift so that the area facing the ground will feel the sinking.

Hands

First, the wrists must be relaxed throughout all movements, maintaining a feeling as if resting. The palms should not be stretched out but held in a naturally open, relaxed manner. The fingers should be extended, but not over-stretched. In the mind, all five fingers touch; but in the actual posture each has a little space in between.

The hand is at the tip of the body's neural network, and it is very sensitive. The hand has been a foundation of our human civilization, and it is our primary tool of action. Instinctively, the first part of the body that begins to move in reaction to an outside stimulus is the hand. For kung-fu, not only must this habit change, it must be reversed. Kung-fu movements must begin with the body (spine and waist), followed by the arms and legs. The shoulder must lead the elbow, the elbow leads the wrist, and the wrist leads the fingers.

If the wrong kind of focus is directed to the hands, interesting reactions such as a nice trembling, heat, or a kind of fullness could occur. Tempting though it may be, you shouldn't jump to congratulate yourself because this is not really the *qi,* or internal energy. In fact, these sensations are quite easy to get and to call them *qi* is misleading, especially while the major body part—the torso—remains inert and untrained.

Knees

The knee, strategically located at the middle of the leg, is a joint of major importance. Even though a human's natural impulse is to pay most attention to the hands and arms, primary focus must shift to the legs. The legs set the pace, propel the action, choose the direction. The arms make their adjustments and move in response to orders from the legs.

The knee, however, is extremely complicated and quite weak. According to an old Chinese saying, "The knee is made of tofu." During training the knee is worked very hard, most of the time in a bent position, putting it under a great deal of stress. The knee's flexibility and degree of movement are limited. It can bend in only one direction and can shift left or right only to a small degree.

Certainly the knee and leg have less flexibility than the elbow and arm, but it occupies a key position in creating the body's foundation. In addition, the arms can rest while they dangle from

The knee, strategically located at the middle of the leg, is a joint of major importance.

the shoulders awaiting the next command to act; but the legs are continually at work even while the body is standing still.

Relaxation can make it easier for the knees to perform their duties. The legs and ankles should coordinate and cooperate completely. In addition, the knee itself must learn to expand beyond its habitual way of moving in daily life—bending, closing, straightening—and incorporate twisting, grinding, and rotating into its repertoire.

Feet

The ankles must be straight and relaxed to cooperate with the feet. Foot movements are usually divided and distributed to the heel, toe, side, and arch. In a single step those areas move in a certain order. The key to controlling the foot, however, is correct ankle management. It is not simply a case of plunking down one component and then the other moves. The ankle moves the foot.

Kung-fu principles instruct you to arch the sole or create some space under the foot. The foot must be relaxed, and not overly straight or artificially flattened. It is a mistake to raise the arch deliberately, contracting and tensing the foot to create some room under the sole. In addition, the toes should grab the ground, but this must also occur in a natural and relaxed manner. You should not intentionally tighten your feet, clench the toes, and force them to grab at the ground. Even without the impediment of shoes and socks, the earth's floor remains beyond the grasp of human toes! More seriously, you can place yourself in a precarious situation because you are robbed of proper balance and leverage needed to create the correct movements and postures.

Follow the basics

The principles outlined in this article are general and basic. Quite naturally, various styles have devised different ways to help students progress to higher levels. Rather than aiming straight for the goal, an indirect route consisting of three to five steps might be employed. Whatever the route, any training that contradicts these basic constitutional principles is wrong.

Kung-fu styles like taijiquan have become widespread and popular. It is important for all practitioners to understand a major weaknesses in the transmission of traditional Chinese arts: a lack of basic training. In fact, step-by-step training programs, standardized terminology, clear explanations, and correct interpretations are either entirely missing or woefully scarce. Chinese painting, music, Beijing Opera, even gourmet cooking all share this condition.

Be on the alert when learning the general rules and movements of kung-fu. Even more importantly, keep an open attitude toward different ideas and interpretations, be willing to compare and experiment, and have the courage to help uphold the kung-fu constitution.

Stance Training

A common feature of kung-fu fiction and movies is the scene where the novice students are diligently practicing their horse stances, silently facing a wall and not daring to make any movement. In fact, this depiction is so common that the Chinese created an expression to characterize this tradition: "Three years for the horse stance." The idea behind this expression is that the practitioner must spend several years auditioning for the instructor by practicing the horse stance.

This expression need not be taken literally today. It does represent the proper attitude necessary for any aspect of kung-fu training, however, and implies that the student must be serious and devoted to the art.

The traditional method of stance training has origins in the culture of ancient China. Before the end of the Qing dynasty (1644–1912), kung-fu was a way of survival, and only through serious, and sometimes dangerous, training and severe testing could a kung-fu practitioner prepare himself for combat. The laws of ancient China were also different than those that govern our modern society. When a major crime—attacking a village or attempting to over-

Stances characteristic of baqua-zhang help practitioners advance within the framework of the style.

throw the government—was committed, the offender and his family were often executed in retribution. If the offender was a kung-fu practitioner, his instructor could also be held responsible and possibly executed.

As a result, instructors were very careful to assess the character of a prospective student, and traditional stance training served as a way to weed out potentially unworthy students. The "three years of horse stance" discouraged students with bad intentions. In addition, it also taught the values of patience, loyalty, and discipline, thus helping to establish the trust and obedience necessary for the proper instructor-student relationship. The student would be able to accept instruction earnestly and without question.

Besides the mental conditioning it provides, stance training is an important tool in conditioning the legs for decisive, powerful footwork.

Besides the mental conditioning it provides, stance training is an important tool in conditioning the legs for decisive, powerful footwork. Kung-fu fighting techniques often require body contact using the shoulders, hips, elbows, and knees, as well as the hands and feet. If the leg foundation is not strong enough, the practitioner cannot fight effectively.

Another aspect of stance training focuses on *qi,* sinking the breath to the *dantian.* While holding each stance, the breath is calm and relaxed. If the breath is strained or uneven, this training may have harmful effects. Correct *qi* training is like accumulating money in the bank: when enough money *(qi)* has been saved, the practitioner can spend some of it (direct the *qi* to different parts of the body). This is a high level that few practitioners reach.

Kung-fu takes a long time to master. By introducing stance training early, students can begin to understand the value of patience in learning the art. The kung-fu approach to fighting, for example, requires a patient attitude. Many practitioners are more inclined to try to take advantage of the first opportunity to act, which may not be the best. While this aggressive attitude is not necessarily bad, it doesn't help in learning the kung-fu way to fight. The kung-fu way is to be patient, waiting for the best opportunity in which the opponent can be totally controlled and completely destroyed.

In contemporary times, instructors don't need to be as concerned with checking the mental and physical qualifications of students. The lifestyle of the modern practitioner is radically different from the ancient monks and farmers who trained in the traditional way.

Having the student face a wall in a low horse stance each day for three years is not the best way to promote kung-fu or to help the student progress.

Some instructors today, however, interpret the "three years of horse stance" expression too literally. Certainly, stance training is an essential part of kung-fu, but the teacher needs to realize that we are not living in a society comparable with ancient China. Stance training should be emphasized in such a way that students feel compelled to take the basics seriously. (No matter what discipline—karate, kendo, ballet, or voice—the basics are less interesting than the forms. How many singers prefer singing scales instead of actual songs?) Having students face a wall in a low horse stance each day for three years is not the best way to promote kung-fu or to help them progress. Some unqualified instructors use excessive stance training to avoid teaching, saying students who are unable to complete the stance training "fail" to qualify to study at their schools.

Students hold kun yu sword form posture.

Given the importance of stance training, we need to adopt more practical ways of teaching stances and other aspects of basic training so students can fully develop their potential. One way to accomplish this is to create a series of stances characteristic of a particular style. In northern style kung-fu, for example, the *ba shi* (eight stances) are practiced. This arrangement of postures helps the student understand the physical mechanics of movement and provides the benefits of traditional stance training. The practitioner holds each posture for as long as possible, without forcing the breath. The transitions between stances also teach the practitioner how to coordinate the body in a single, unified motion.

Using this model, instructors can develop their own *ba shi*. For instance, *ru huan shi* (twisting and sitting stance) is an important stance in the praying mantis system. By including this and other basic stances in a sequence, the special features of the praying mantis style can be utilized. It's not necessary to have eight stances only; the number may be more or less, depending on the structure of the kung-fu style. Another way to vary stance training and make it more interesting for the student is to hold certain postures in forms. Changquan, for example, has a great deal of kicking. In the style's basic line form, *tan tui,* the student can hold each kick in the air for a few breaths. In bajiquan, the student is required to hold each stance for a specific number of breaths.

This type of training could be applied to the first form of any style, such as taijiquan. All instructors should examine their training methods and try to develop ways to creatively incorporate stance training into their art. In this way, students will be assured the benefits of basic training and will also develop a better understanding of kung-fu.

Kung-fu's Way to Power

Even small children understand that the larger the working distance one has, the greater the power one can generate. Children learn early on that in order to throw a ball far they need to start the throw from behind their shoulder. Then the arm and hand pass over (in the case of an overhand throw) the shoulder, and finally as the ball is released the arm follows through in front of the body. In this way the ball is thrown much farther than if merely flicked by the wrist or using the elbow and forearm. Similarly, one does not try to pound in a nail with the hammer held an inch away. The farther the hammer is held away from the nail the harder the nail can be struck. These are obvious examples of increasing one's working distance to allow for greater power.

However, because our bodies are limited, it follows that our working distance is also limited. We can move our arm or leg only a certain distance. Even the largest person has limitations. Therefore, we try other ways to heighten our power. One, we try to increase our strength. Two, we try to increase our speed. Kung-

The chan si jin technique initiates at the foot, then uses the ankle, knee, hip, waist, back, shoulder, elbow, wrist, and finally the hand.

fu and all martial art systems recognize the necessity of speed and strength in technique, and train to develop these qualities. Another part of kung-fu training, though, is to develop a different way of moving in order to increase the working distance.

This unique way of moving the body is called *chan si jin* (reeling silk energy). It is a spiraling rather than straight movement, and has been understood in China since ancient times. In the ancient farming culture family roles were clearly defined. The men worked the fields, and the women primarily stayed at home. Among the women's chores was the reeling of silk, removing the silk from the silkworms' cocoons. As they pulled the silk, the cocoon would spin. This act of reeling silk, called *chan si* in Chinese, was a part of everyday life; all were familiar with it. The spiraling effect of reeling silk was very much like the kung-fu way of using the body in order to issue power. Hence, *chan si jin* was taken as the name of this kung-fu technique.

Today, machinery has replaced what was once done by hand, and the old way of reeling silk is no longer part of everyday life. Therefore, the term *chan si jin* is now difficult for many people to understand. Where once the instructors used the term to help people understand the kung-fu way of issuing power, now it seems rather obscure and mysterious.

The kung-fu way is to get the whole body involved in the *chan si jin*. This is not a natural style of movement or means of generating power. Based on our experience we have all acquired our own ways of utilizing our body to assist us in getting power. Consciously and unconsciously we

The spiraling effect of reeling silk was very much like the kung-fu way of using the body in order to issue power.

have developed styles and habits through work, sports, and everyday life that we are reliant on. None of these are the kung-fu way.

To learn a difficult and sophisticated technique such as *chan si jin* takes great patience and a step-by-step approach. The first step is to shed old habits. That is why the instructor teaches the beginning student over and over again to relax when practicing. In order to learn a new way of moving, students must become aware of their old ways. The teacher first tells the student not to try and use power, because not yet knowing better the student would naturally revert to the old way of moving. Initially, the student must practice slowly and relax to create an opportunity for the *chan si jin* to develop.

Some students, although claiming to be studying kung-fu, do not adhere to the correct way of practicing. These people, for various reasons such as impatience, frustration, or lack of faith, choose not to practice "without" power. Some of them are young and strong and can already issue some power. Unfortunately, they are cheating themselves and can easily destroy their own potential to reach a high level of kung-fu. *Chan si jin* is a high-level technique that depends on hard work, correct practice, and the guidance of a qualified instructor.

You might ask in what way a martial artist can use this vague concept of *chan si jin*. Using *chan si jin* in punching, for example, involves the entire body, not just the shoulder and arm. The technique initiates at the foot, then uses the ankle, knee, hip, waist, back, shoulder, elbow, wrist, and finally the hand. All of the body's joints are applied in a highly disciplined twisting action. In other words, each joint, beginning with the ankle and toes, is twisting, not only individually, but all working together as a single unit.

Tomb of bagua founder Dong Hai Quan. In the 1980s his body was exhumed from an obscure grave and reburied with full honors in the specially-built Beijing monument.

The effect is a spiraling accumulation of power from the ground up. Using the fist as its vehicle, the accumulated power of the entire body is thus issued to a single, focused point.

The practitioner who can really use *chan si jin* can issue great power. The working distance covers the length of the body from heel to hand. However, this distance is not to be measured as a straight line. We would need to measure the distance via the curved line of the spiral. Using *chan si jin* the practitioner's working distance becomes tremendously large.

It has often seemed an unexplainable phenomenon that certain instructors of unimposing physique are able to issue great power. People have wondered how it is done. Is it through supernatural power, illusion, mind over matter? The actual explanation is not so arcane. It is the result of years of difficult and serious training, of training the body to work in an extraordinarily effective way—a way that the ancients likened to women's reeling of silk, *chan si jin.*

How Much Flexibility is Enough for Kung-fu

Any type of exercise requires a certain amount of flexibility. For the multitude of martial arts, flexibility plays an especially critical role. The body is used as a weapon to attack and defend, and therefore must be both flexible and relaxed to initiate any type of movement necessary in an instant.

When we are young our bodies are soft and pliable. Although we get stronger and accustomed to more complicated movement as we age, we usually lose a great deal of our natural flexibility. This is one reason martial arts teachers so often strongly advocate beginning training at an early age; it makes it easier for students to reach their goals with regard to becoming sufficiently flexible.

The role of flexibility training in kung-fu is often greatly exaggerated and is largely misunderstood, however. Some instructors overemphasize stretching. This approach stems from their own misconceptions about the actual function and origin of stretching. Some unfortunate instructors may focus on stretching as a substitute for lacking enough real kung-fu techniques to teach students.

I believe that it is wrong for any teacher to demand that every student achieve the same level of flexibility. Many factors other than stretching itself have an influence on flexibility, including the person's age, body type, and athletic background. Practitioners who cannot reach the maximum degree of body flexibility can develop into fine martial artists. Leg strength, overall conditioning, and diligent and intelligent practice all help compensate for a lack of flexibility.

In fact, stretching too much can actually destroy a student's kung-fu foundation. By stretching too much, the muscle becomes too long and possibly too soft. This condition makes it difficult for a practitioner to issue power correctly. A certain amount of dynamic tension and a great deal of leg strength are needed to fully generate the power from the lower body. Flexibility should not be confused with leg strength, one is not a replacement for the other. The two should develop concurrently.

By stretching too much, the muscle becomes too long and possibly too soft, making it difficult for a practitioner to issue power correctly.

In addition, recovering from over-stretching is much more difficult than becoming more flexible when a practitioner is under-stretched. Flexibility training should be treated as simply another integral part of the overall kung-fu training and conditioning program, not as something special unto itself.

Today we see that many kung-fu forms contain and are judged by the many acrobatic and flexibility-inspired techniques and postures they contain. Granted, these are in fact often difficult to execute, yet some teachers mistakenly include and overuse these types of movements as evidence of having achieved a high level in kung-fu.

Unfortunately, when the majority of people think of kung-fu, the forms and techniques mentioned come to mind. It is through observing the acrobatic and dance-like forms that many martial artists judge the integrity and viability of kung-fu as a whole. This is why many hold the opinion that kung-fu is not effective as a fighting art. These forms exhibit good

A certain amount of dynamic tension and a great deal of leg strength are needed to fully generate the power from the lower body.

conditioning and balance perhaps, but certainly not superior kung-fu technique as many have come to believe.

Perhaps the following analogy can place the role and importance of stretching and flexibility into a clearer perspective. A singer usually begins training by singing the basic scale of notes. At this early stage, of course, the full range of these notes will not be at the novice's command, just as in stretching we have a natural range of flexibility with which we begin. But, through diligent practice, the singer's range will eventually expand to include the entire range of notes, a feat that previously had been quite impossible. Similarly, students who stretch correctly and persistently will also achieve a wider range of flexibility and movement.

Yet, when an accomplished singer sings a song, the vocal range required is less than what was encompassed in the training. But this basic training was indeed necessary and valuable, because it covered all the possibilities and provided the singer with a stronger and wider base from which to sing a broader variety of songs.

Also, as any singer will tell you, just because one can sing the basic notes does not automatically guarantee that one can sing a song both correctly and artistically. Elements such as emotion, rhythm, and tempo must also be included to make the song truly complete and convincing. Similarly, many other skills must be combined with flexibility training in order to achieve real proficiency in kung-fu.

Remaining at this "flexibility is kung-fu" level, and confusing it with real kung-fu expertise, is like perpetually singing just the basic range of notes and promoting that as an outstanding piece of music. Ultimately, kung-fu requires a great deal more than the capability to perform movements loosely and gracefully.

Part 3

Myth and Reality of Kung-fu Styles

The Real Difference Between Internal and External Kung-fu

Generally speaking, we can point to the end of the Ming dynasty (1368–1644) and the beginning of the Qing dynasty (1644–1911) as the time in China when misconceptions regarding internal and external kung-fu first arose. At that time Huang Li-Chou, a famous Chinese writer, philosopher, and underground army leader, maintained strong opposition against the Manchus, who were responsible for the overthrow of the Ming and the establishment of Qing in its place.

I greatly respect Huang's ideas and unshakable convictions concerning loyalty and the preservation of Chinese traditions, as well as his courageous resistance against the Manchus. I cannot agree, however, with one of his essays in which he attempts to clarify the distinction between internal and external kung-fu, unduly assigning the internal more value and a greater importance.

During the 300 years of the Qing dynasty, Huang's internal/external viewpoint did little to change the quality and conceptions of Chinese kung-fu. At that time kung-fu was still a practical and extremely serious art because of the rule and occupation of China by the Manchus.

Toward the end of the Qing dynasty, the appearance of the European nations, equipped with ships, cannon, and rifles, seriously compromised not only the power and influence of the Qing government but the credibility in combat of kung-fu as well. The Chinese people realized the limits of kung-fu's effectiveness on the battlefield against modern arsenals.

The period between the end of the Qing dynasty and the beginning of the Republic marked a turning point in the evolution of kung-fu, which even until today is largely responsible for how most people conceive of Chinese martial arts. At this time, some well educated and less physically qualified people applied their philosophies as a substitute for lack of real kung-fu technique. The great respect accorded Huang's insightful writings against the Qing dynasty unfortunately carried over to his erroneous work on external and internal kung-fu.

Many of the authors of kung-fu books were never respected in real kung-fu circles

Taijiquan, baguazhang, and xingyiquan were all classified as the popular internal styles. The credibility of this was, and still is, upheld by conveniently pointing to ancient and highly esteemed religious and moral philosophies that shared similar terminology but were totally unrelated to martial arts in any other way.

Scholars in China often use the writings and philosophies of famous people to give credence to and help perpetuate their own ideas. And in this case, after a short time, it appeared as if the distinction between internal/external kung-fu had always existed. Many books that were written to justify this connection have been translated into other languages and have been responsible for

The author with one of his taijiquan classes in Taipei, Taiwan.

spreading a great deal of misinformation. Many of the authors of kung-fu books were never respected in real kung-fu circles, but only by those who lacked the skill and expertise to tell the difference.

As kung-fu was now no longer emphasized as a fighting art, many dishonest and unqualified people had an opportunity to use kung-fu as a way to deceive the public. Capitalizing on this new trend, they assured people that their kung-fu was internal and that one never needed to exert oneself to become powerful and skillful. Many people, unwilling to endure the pains and rigorous demands of real training, naturally flocked to these fantasy-like promises—and thus the myth extended even further.

These so-called internal styles often claim that they practice very softly and comfortably. They don't work on free sparring or train for speed and power in their techniques, insisting that it is not necessary for them because of the enormous amount of internal power they have accumulated. Other more amazing internal claims include being able to defeat an opponent without touching him, or even harming one's opponent by taking the force of his technique and immediately sending it back against him. I know for a fact that most of these demonstrations of internal power are made possible by gimmicks.

Often these practitioners cannot prove their power against non-believers or give substantiated proof about stories regarding their own connection with adepts who lived around the time of the late Qing and early Republic period. I have met with these genuine older practitioners, however, and only very few claim to have an extraordinary ability; most admit that the stories of their spectacular feats are quite ridiculous and exaggerated. I do admit there are a few people who can legitimately tap this unknown power, but as remarkable as it may appear, it is not remarkable kung-fu.

A wide variety of interesting and contradictory explanations were developed concerning just what was internal and external. A few are mentioned here:

• Shaolin is external because it was a Buddhist temple and Buddhism came from the outside (external) into China. Wu Tang is internal because it is Taoist and Taoism is a product of China.

- Wu Tang is external because the highest Taoist training seeks immortality and transcendence of human affairs. Shaolin is internal because of the monks' use of the *Internal Buddhist Bible*, a religious book.
- Any hard or fast movements are external; soft and slower movements are internal.
- Overpowering and destroying the enemy in application is external; neutralizing and using the opponent's energy against him is internal.
- Kung-fu with lots of movements is external; simpler, more comfortable movements are internal.
- Making a sound while practicing is external; quiet kung-fu is internal because all energy is concentrated inside one's body.
- Silent kung-fu is external because breathing was not practiced along with the movements; noisy kung-fu is internal because the sound and the breathing move in unison.

Sound confusing? It is!

After World War II these ways of categorizing kung-fu moved out of China and into the Western world. Since the end of the Qing dynasty, kung-fu has changed greatly. Few real techniques have been completely and accurately passed down because of three main reasons. First, instructors traditionally held back because of secrecy and safety. Second, there was the belief that because of firearms, martial arts were no longer necessary. Many kung-fu men, facing the change in times, were unable or unwilling to adjust. With their integrity and personal value shattered, they became casualties of their time. Lastly, since kung-fu was traditionally viewed as mostly a martial art, few people at that time saw its peaceful potential as an art, health exercise, or form of meditation.

In Chinese, the words used for external and internal are *wai* and *nei* respectively. Chinese people never would willingly like to be referred to as *wai hang* or *men wai hang,* which means an outsider, amateurish, unskilled. Because of these connotations, everyone naturally wanted to be considered *nei* or internal. It was always the other people who were *wai,* external, outside. And through rumors, jealousies, and rivalries, many confusing and contradictory viewpoints concerning internal and external spread.

When kung-fu came to America, students adopted many of their instructors' prejudices and misconceptions. In many cases, by not clearly understanding the use of internal and external in Chinese culture, students began to create their own explanations as to what the differences were. Needless to say, this added to an already confusing and unclear situation.

Internal and external do not represent different styles or kinds of kung-fu, but rather different levels.

I believe that all these internal/external theories are in fact quite incorrect. The distinction is really very simple to understand. Internal and external do not represent different styles or kinds of kung-fu, but rather different levels. We can say that the external represents the lower or more elementary level of kung-fu, and the internal the higher and more complex. Therefore in real kung-fu training, regardless of the style, one must begin from the external and patiently and systematically progress inward to the internal.

Since some instructors were unable to complete the entire training in their particular styles, many systems today are incomplete and never go beyond the external level. If practitioners are carefully guided by an honest and qualified teacher, who went through the complete training in a certain style, they will move step-by-step from the outside, through the door, climb upstairs to the top level, and then reach the internal—the highest level of kung-fu.

The Myth of Shaolin Kung-fu

The Shaolin Temple is often thought of as the origin and center of martial arts. The Shaolin monks passed on their ancient arts, providing the seeds from which the numerous kung-fu styles grew over the centuries. In reality, Shaolin kung-fu is mostly a fairy tale, and the origins of Shaolin kung-fu is more mythical than real.

In reality, Shaolin kung-fu is mostly a fairy tale, and the origins of Shaolin kung-fu is more mythical than real.

It is said that the Shaolin Temple was a Zen Buddhist temple. This is accurate, but for the most part the truth about Shaolin ends here. We are told monk Ta Mo came to China from India during the Liang dynasty (A.D. 506–56), Southern and Northern Kingdoms Period (A.D. 420–589), with the intention of teaching Buddhism. Ta Mo wanted to get to northern China, so upon reaching the Yangtze River, he allegedly crossed it on a reed. After arriving at the Shaolin Temple, he meditated for nine years facing a wall. Ta Mo taught his fellow monks Buddhism, but he felt they were not healthy enough. To remedy this situation, he taught the monks a martial art he had brought with him from India. This was supposedly the beginning of Shaolin kung-fu.

The tale goes on to say that all Shaolin monks received serious kung-fu training. The monks reached a high level of proficiency in their skills, and the temple became famous for its kung-fu. Monks who were not good enough, and those who could not endure the harsh training, were kicked out of the temple. Though these ostracized monks did not meet the temple's standards, once they were in society, their kung-fu was considered incomparable.

Let's examine these fairy tales. To say that kung-fu began with Ta Mo during the Liang dynasty is to ignore a good portion of Chinese history. We need go no further back than Huang Ti to verify that organized warfare and martial arts were firmly established in China at least hundreds of years before Ta Mo's arrival. During the Spring Autumn Period (722–481 B.C.) and the Warring States Period (475–221 B.C.), hundreds of wars occurred in China. Knowledge of warfare and fighting technique were under continuous development. Weapons unceasingly changed and improved. Professional soldiers were employed, war scholars compiled data, criteria for selection of soldiers was established, and the chariot gave way to the horse cavalry.

Students performing on the streets of Deng Feng City, China, during the 1991 Shaolin Wushu Festival.

Furthermore, in the Spring Autumn Period, Kwang Tzu used a draft to assemble capable martial artists for his army. Also, *Han Shu,* a book recording the history of the Han dynasty (206 B.C.–A.D. 200), shows sections in its index on battle knowledge and martial arts.

Still further evidence of the existence of martial arts before Ta Mo can be seen from accounts of the famous King Wei Wen Ti of the Three Kingdoms Period (A.D. 211–65). King Wei wanted to test his sword skill against General Den Tzan. Den was renown for his bare-hand fighting skill against weapons. To this day the phrase *"kong shou ru bei ren"* (bare-hand versus weapon) is associated with General Den. After a banquet, King Wei and General Den dueled. So as not to actually kill each other, they fought with lengths of sugarcane rather than swords. The contest ended with Wei striking Den on the forehead. This episode proves that martial arts skill was so pervasive that even kings possessed it.

Now let's look at the assertion that Ta Mo crossed the

Yangtze River on a reed. The Chinese character for small boat is *wei*. A similar Chinese character is pronounced identically, but this character means reed. Because many martial artists at the time were poorly educated, even illiterate, they mistook the character which means small boat for reed. Thus this fantastic idea, that Ta Mo crossed the Yangtze River on a reed took hold and supported the belief that he possessed supernatural powers.

There are so many homonyms in the Chinese language that it is not unusual for one character to be mistaken for another, especially by poorly educated people. Two such examples appear in the poem "The Wide River," taken from the *Shi Jing (Book of Songs)*, an anthology of poems compiled by Confucius. In the verse "Who says the Yellow River is wide/A small boat can cross it," the character *wei* (small boat) is, as in the Ta Mo legend, misconstrued to mean reed. And in another verse, "Who says the Yellow River is wide/A small boat can't even fit in it," the character *tao* (also meaning small boat) is sometimes mistaken for its homonym *tao,* which means saber.

I do not debate that Shaolin was a famous Zen temple. Whether Ta Mo taught exercises at the temple, however, can be neither proven nor disproven because there is not enough evidence. Prior to Ta Mo's arrival at the Shaolin Temple, there were monks who had already mastered kung-fu. Many of the monks at Shaolin were men who originally came to the temple seeking refuge. Some of these men were killers, rapists, and thieves. Once, however, they were accepted by the temple as monks, and if their crime had not been of the unpardonable sort (such as treason) they would no longer be hunted. This type of man often had some kung-fu technique, and the temple was an ideal place for working on it.

The monks lived simply and, not having to worry about making a living, they had plenty of time to practice kung-fu. The dictates of Buddhism governed the temple; killing was not tolerated. Within this unusual environment the monks could get together and, respectfully and without fear, exchange their kung-fu knowledge. Over the years, the kung-fu at Shaolin may very well have improved and become more sophisticated, but at no time was the Shaolin Temple considered a kung-fu school. To assert that kung-fu originated there with Ta Mo is absurd. The Chinese brought kung-fu to the Shaolin Temple and, before that, it had already been practiced throughout China for hundreds of years.

The most famous weapon of the Shaolin Temple was the staff. This fact helps to illustrate that Shaolin was a Buddhist school, not a kung-fu school. No weapons were kept in the temple. Machine guns and missiles aren't stored in churches; likewise, weapons were not allowed in a Buddhist temple. The most famous weapon practiced at Shaolin was the staff because it was the only weapon available to the monks.

During the Tang dynasty (A.D. 618–907), the Shaolin monks received recognition for helping the government put down a rebellion. For their assistance, the monks were rewarded by the king, and the temple held an honored place in society.

After the Tang dynasty, numerous civil wars were fought. These outbreaks ranged from small skirmishes to serious battles. Although many martial artists were involved, it is not known whether or not the Shaolin Temple ever played a part in these conflicts. It is recorded, however, that a few individuals claimed to be from the Shaolin Temple.

We can continue down through history to the Ming dynasty (A.D. 1368–1644), an important period in kung-fu history. The

The author visits the Pagoda Forest, ancient burial grounds for Shaolin monks.

eminent General Che Chi Kwong did extensive research on kung-fu in order to help train his soldiers. General Che wrote a book, and in it listed all the good and famous kung-fu styles of his day. There is no mention of Shaolin.

Until the Qing dynasty (A.D. 1644–1912), Shaolin was neither emphasized nor popular. But at this point in history the name Shaolin began to be known. One reason for this is that the secret societies aligned themselves with Shaolin. These underground organizations arose in response to the Manchu government, which they wanted to overthrow. The societies flourished primarily in the south, far from the power base of the Manchus in the north. They emphasized Shaolin because the Shaolin Temple was located in the north, within the immediate influence of the Manchus. This implied that the secret societies were challenging the rulers where they were strongest. Also, an alignment with Shaolin, a Buddhist temple, helped to foster within the societies a sense of holy purpose.

Another reason Shaolin became known during the Qing dynasty is because of the popular *Sword-Man* fictions. In these tales, Shaolin was portrayed as a major kung-fu system. According to the *Sword-Man* fictions, there were branches of Shaolin in Fukien, Guangdong, Siquan, and other provinces. Actually, there was only one, in Henan, and it has been reopened to tourists.

I have checked lots of *fang zhi* (local records) of all the cities that the *Sword-Man* fictions mention as locations of a Shaolin Temple. I've also talked to people from these areas. There is no mention of Shaolin in any of the *fang zhi* (except Henan's), and no one I've talked to knows anything about a Shaolin Temple in their respective hometowns.

A third reason for the propagation of Shaolin during the Qing dynasty was the kung-fu *sifu*. Once the name of Shaolin became popular, these men were quick to capitalize on it. They cared little about misconceptions and misunderstandings; they needed to make a living. If Shaolin kung-fu attracted students, these *sifu* claimed their system descended from it.

To this day many instructors claim to teach Shaolin. However, when I was in training, I met no one who could define

Shaolin kung-fu. Mostly what is referred to as Shaolin is actually the long fist system (changquan). Long fist has many styles; it is the broadest system in kung-fu. No instructor could prove that what they were teaching came directly from Shaolin. Interestingly, one very popular style of long fist, jia men, comes from the Chinese Muslims. Jia men is still being practiced in northern China.

Today, as in the past, Shaolin kung-fu is less respected in northern China than in southern China. Starting from the end of the Qing dynasty, many instructors moved down to the Yangtze River area. For advertising reasons they emphasized Shaolin. During World War II, these instructors moved further south to Guangzhou and Hong Kong, continuing to use Shaolin to help their business. Overseas Chinese have spread the Shaolin myth to the U.S. and other countries. Ironically, there is more Shaolin kung-fu in southern China than in Henan Province itself.

In 1928 the Chinese government established in Nanking the Central Government Martial Arts Institute. Initially, the institute helped sustain the Shaolin myth, offering departments in Shaolin and Wu Tang. A member of the staff, Tang Hao, was uncomfortable with this situation. To clarify the misconceptions about Shaolin and Wu Tang, Tang Hao wrote a book titled *The Study of Shaolin and Wu Tang.* It is a good book, based on honest research. However, it was written elegantly, in classical Chinese. This made it inaccessible to many people, especially the martial artists. The book is also difficult to translate into a foreign language. After the

Young Shaolin students performing the Temple's most famous weapon: the staff.

publication of Tang's book, the institute changed its policies on Shaolin and Wu Tang.

Even though this book was published almost six decades ago, and since then lots of other evidence refuting the Shaolin myth has surfaced, people still persist with their fairy tales. I want to make clear that I'm not saying kung-fu did not exist at the Shaolin Temple. I believe kung-fu was practiced there; there is evidence of it in paintings, poems, and in the temple itself. I also agree that the Shaolin Temple helped the government during the Tang dynasty. In the evolution of kung-fu, however, Shaolin kung-fu holds little importance. Shaolin didn't even develop its own style. What is really ridiculous, though, is to pretend that Shaolin is the birthplace of kung-fu. It is time to stop calling what may be a grandchild the grandfather.

In the evolution of kung-fu, Shaolin kung-fu holds little importance.

The Internal Dilemma

It's not unusual to find a kung-fu practitioners with a true love of the art, strong curiosity, dedication, and willingness to work hard standing lost at a crossroads. They can't decide which avenue to take: xingyiquan, taijiquan, or baguazhang.

They want to study all three arts because they are told that one must master all three to maintain the true, high levels of internal kung-fu.

Which one provides the best starting point? Which one should be the final step?

Adding to the confusion, few instructors are available who can teach all three arts. Moreover, the really good teachers focus on one style. So what path to take?

First, we must eliminate the misconception surrounding so-called internal styles. All martial artists must start with tough fundamental training and possess a fair amount of athletic ability. This is the external part of training. High-level techniques are possible only when built upon the foundation of strong basics. Higher levels use less rough power, more mature techniques, and must engage the mind and spirit. This we call internal kung-fu.

The truth is that any style can be an internal style but not every practitioner can reach levels high enough to earn the distinction of internal stylist even if they practice taiji, xingyi, or bagua.

Kung-fu styles have unique flavors stemming from a different emphasis on straightforward or circular motion. Therefore, nothing can substitute for extensive hands-on exposure to help judge what is best for the individual.

Sometimes a preference comes directly from the heart and cannot be explained. Sometimes it relates to personality and character. It can also be influenced by physical habits developed from work, sports, or everyday life. In making the choice, however, you alone are master. You should not force yourself to fit a certain great style just to fulfill a desire. Xingyi, bagua, and taiji are all great styles. If you choose one that doesn't suit you, why not switch to another that gives you the chance the reach a high level of accomplishment.

Although choice of the style belongs to the practitioner, finding a style that totally suits one's abilities and interests may be difficult. In this situation a lesson can be learned from the modern university system. The style closest to an ideal can be a major. Studying the elements of other styles as a minor can help eliminate weak points and improve the major style.

Studying the elements of other styles as a minor can help eliminate weak points and improve the major style.

Choosing a major and minor is not uncommon. Many xingyi teachers also study bagua. Many taiji teachers have previously studied or mastered other styles. The distinguishing factor is that almost all of these masters reach a high level before switching to another style. However, few have the resources or talent to be the master of more than one style.

Those attracted to xingyi, bagua, and taiji should study the style most suited to them, and stick with it. Don't be duped by those who proclaim that unless you learn all three so-called internal styles you cannot attain a high level. Gather information and sample the different arts. Don't substitute fantasy for hard work. In this way, one may someday cross the threshold to the internal levels and achieve the highest state of the art.

The Dividing Line Between Northern and Southern Styles

A number of martial arts practitioners and historians might be familiar with the popular kung-fu expression *"nan quan, bei tui,"* which translates to "south fists, north legs." The misconceptions surrounding this phrase can be traced back to the founding of the Chinese Republic (1911) when the practice of kung-fu was becoming less vital to Chinese society, and for the first time literature discussing philosophical and technical aspects of various systems of the art began to proliferate.

Despite the fact that many writers of this early period were skilled in a literary sense, their kung-fu expertise was often mediocre at best. It was this lack of true experience and understanding that led them to interpret *"nan quan, bei tui"* literally, meaning that the southern styles emphasized the fist while the northerners used the legs extensively for kicking and jumping.

> *Kung-fu men . . . were not well educated, and many were unable to read or even write their own names.*

In those days, kung-fu men for the most part were not well educated, and many were unable to read or even write their names. It is therefore understandable why such individuals paid little attention to what was published. They believed more in the reality of the sword than the magic of the brush.

But even for those who were literate, the meaning of many of these writings still evaded their understanding. A good number of the writers of that time, because of their strong educational background and training, often utilized various special literary techniques to give their works a more stylistic and meaningful structure.

As an example, one such widely used technique, called *hu wen zhu yi,* embeds another meaning in addition to what appears at face value. It is only through their proper combination of the words that the greater meaning of the phrase surfaces. For example, in *Da Xue (The Great Learning,* one of the four Confucian classics) there is a saying: "Men have jobs, women have marriage *(nan you fen, niu you gui)*." Does this really mean (as it appears and is often interpreted) that men should only work and women only think of marriage? If so, who do the women marry? And what about the men? Are they concerned only with work?

The assumption that leg and kicking techniques dominate so-called northern styles of kung-fu is utterly ridiculous.

Unlike some other Chinese idiomatic literary forms, the word order in *"nan you fen, niu you gui"* is not rigidly fixed. It can also be read *"nan you gui, niu you fen"* (men have marriage, women have work). Through this other interpretation, the overall meaning is enlarged. Men and women are used to represent all people collectively. In the old agricultural society, it was essential for both sexes to work: men usually farmed while the women often wove cloth. And early marriage was strongly encouraged so couples could have large families. Waiting too long would make it more difficult to bear many children since a village needed as many people as possible to help with production and protection against outsiders.

"Nan quan, bei tui" is another example the *hu wen zhu yi* idiomatic form. It can also be read *"nan tui, bei quan"* or "south legs, north fists." Hung-gar and Choy Lay Fut, for example, are two

popular southern kung-fu styles that make extensive use of the legs for kicking and have wide-open postures (another so-called characteristic of only northern styles). On the other hand, there are northern kung-fu styles such as xingyiquan and baguazhang that in comparison make little use of kicking and have narrow and shorter postures and stances—qualities supposedly found only in southern styles.

To say that kung-fu is a complex and sophisticated martial art really means that it is very evenly balanced. Both the upper and lower parts of the body are used in a coordinated and highly disciplined manner. Therefore, should a martial artist be led to believe that as an effective fighting system southern styles use only the hands, as in Western boxing, and that in the north, legs are exclusively used? Even famous Asian martial arts such as taekwondo still incorporate a variety of hand techniques.

Classifying the hundreds of Chinese kung-fu styles into northern and southern makes the issue less complicated for most people and has therefore emerged as the most popular method of categorization. However, kung-fu has also been divided into three groups: the Yellow River region, representing northern styles; the Pearl River region, representing southern styles; and the Yangtze River region, to include all those systems in between. One might well ask: If the northern styles use the legs and the southern the fists, what does the middle area use— the behind?

The purpose of this discussion is to point out that the real kung-fu practitioner has little time for such classification systems. One must

The wild goose feather saber (yen ling dao) *is a rare kung-fu weapon that has the characteristics of both saber and double-edged sword.*

have enough experience and expertise in classical Chinese reading and writing to be able to correctly understand and fully appreciate the unique idiomatic forms. The writers skillfully and artfully combined various literary and rhetorical devices not to make their works simple or enjoyable for the average person. Their primary goals was to satisfy the group of intellectuals who could comprehend and appreciate such works.

Each style has its own characteristic specialty and other aspects that help distinguish it from other styles.

Kung-fu practitioners should instead be concerned with improving and perfecting their own chosen styles. Although the words in *"nan quan, bei tui"* can be changed to *"nan tui, bei quan,"* understanding is still limited without the realization that in Chinese kung-fu the whole arm, and even more so, the whole body is used as a fist. The assumption that legs *(tui)* and kicking techniques dominate so-called northern styles of kung-fu is utterly ridiculous. An experienced practitioner, no matter what style, clearly understands that the leg is not only to be used to support the body, create good balance, and to kick, but more importantly to change the angles of attack and defense and also to control and overpower an enemy.

Regardless of whether one is talking about northern or southern or even "middle" styles, the most attractive and visible movements are naturally the hands, while the leg usage is far less glamorous and remains for the most part hidden. Each style has its own characteristic specialty and other aspects that help distinguish it from the others. Yet, when examining and considering the roots of the basic kung-fu principles and concepts, you'll see the underlying thread that unifies all styles, regardless of the more obvious, outward forms or superficial classifications. Good kung-fu is just good kung-fu.

Should the Many Be One?

Many kung-fu instructors still have a traditional attitude. They insist on holding on to their special art like a treasure that only a privileged few may glimpse. On the other hand, some instructors are more progressive. They want kung-fu to become more fully developed, preserving the ancient tradition so future generations can benefit from that skill and knowledge.

The author, with coach Liu Chang-Chiang, demonstrates the rare Chen thunder style taijiquan in Wang Ge Dang, China—the village of the style's origin.

Some of this latter group even go so far to say that kung-fu should be unified into one style. This would be a single, comprehensive system that includes the fundamental techniques from every kung-fu style. Those who advocate this idea, however, really don't comprehend the nature of the art. To understand why kung-fu would not be improved by integrating the multitude of styles, we need to understand why kung-fu has so many of them.

Three reasons account for the large number of kung-fu styles. First, China is a big country with an extensive history spanning thousands of years. Quite naturally a wide variety of cultures and races exist within the vast provinces of China, and each has its own traditions. Likewise, so does kung-fu. In ancient times each county or village may have had its own style, emphasizing some special technique or weapon. Even today, the southeast villages of Cang county in Hebei province, for example, are still famous for bajiquan and piquazhang. Chen-style taijiquan was almost unknown outside of the Chen family village in Henan Province until the last few decades.

Further variations resulted from foreigners who invaded China throughout its history. The indigenous people frequently mixed with non-natives. As a result, physical characteristics influencing the basic formation of a style vary among the Chinese people. The minorities who inhabit regions of China, such as the Miao in the southwest or the Hui in the northwest, also have their own unique kung-fu styles.

Secondly, kung-fu is a personalized, creative art. The styles were developed out of the experience, abilities, and needs of individuals who depended on their martial skills for survival. In some instances, an instructor with extensive training in several styles of kung-fu formulated a new one consisting of techniques adapted from others. Tanglang (praying mantis), for example, was developed in Shandong province during the Ming dynasty by Wong Long, and is a compilation of various systems.

At that time some martial arts in China had become dance-like and impractical. It is said Wong Long blended techniques from 18 styles to develop tanglang as an effective fighting method emphasizing practical application. At the other extreme, styles such as baguazhang or piquazhang seem to have no clearly definable antecedents. The techniques and flavor of these styles are unlike those of any other. They reflect the founder's unique personality.

Instructors trained in a specific kung-fu tradition will also have a personal fighting technique that emphasizes a particular aspect of the style. They may have followers who learn the art, taking over their specialty, or they might help students to develop their own specialties. As a result, even within one style different branches exist, some without any special name. Changquan (long fist), for example, consists of many branches, including jia men (Islamic), mei hua (plum blossom), and taizhu (grand ancestor).

The third reason for the vast number of styles involves the nature of kung-fu itself. Kung-fu is a flexible art. There are general principles that must be followed, but kung-fu doesn't try to force practitioners into a fixed, rigid shape that limits the possibilities for technique and usage. As in the Chinese theory of *yin* and *yang,* the techniques are not rigid but easily changeable, adaptable to the situation. The multitude of styles provides a way to accommodate the needs and abilities of individual practitioners.

The multitude of styles provides a way to accommodate the needs and abilities of individual practitioners.

The existence of so many styles is an unavoidable reality, but it is not the most ideal situation. Many styles and techniques are similar, and some styles do not have a complete training system. If the number were reduced by eliminating styles lacking the substance that comprises a kung-fu system, the art as a whole could be refined and further developed. Even so, kung-fu would still have more styles than any other martial art.

A wholesale restructuring of kung-fu, however, would not save it, but ultimately destroy it. Each style has a unique personality that may not mix harmoniously with other styles. For kung-fu to survive, all the legitimate techniques and styles must be preserved, otherwise the quality and integrity of the art will suffer.

Another point to consider is that a unified kung-fu system would require one to master all the major techniques gathered from every style. Determining how to choose which techniques are preserved and which are discarded would be a problem. This issue would create an endless controversy among instructors. Even if it were possible to create a unified kung-fu style through the research of an expert committee or with the aid of computers, the mass of techniques would nevertheless eventually form into groups and separate styles again. Additionally, this approach would limit the practitioner's potential to become skilled. If the choice of styles is limited, fewer people will be able to benefit from kung-fu.

Rather than putting effort into unifying the styles of the art, effort should be made toward unifying kung-fu instructors in an association where ideas can be exchanged and some general standards can be established in order to insure that the basic character is maintained. Training at the most fundamental levels, for example, could be standardized, which would not affect or limit the special techniques and training of any particular style.

An international kung-fu organization could also arrange for an objective and safe way to compete in both fighting and forms, and establish a ranking system similar to that used by the Japanese martial arts. I would suggest both a general ranking for kung-fu and a ranking for each specific style. The general ranking would entail all the fundamental techniques and training, and the style ranking would relate to the techniques, usage, and forms of the practitioner's specific system. I would like to hear practitioners introducing themselves as X-level kung-fu, X-level xingyiquan, for example.

Rather than putting effort into unifying the styles of the art, effort should be made toward unifying kung-fu instructors.

The many styles will definitely not be improved by becoming one system, but the many instructors could improve the art by uniting in an effort to create standards for future generations of kung-fu practitioners.

A Lifelong Commitment to One Style

The wide variety of kung-fu styles is a great bounty. Kung-fu practitioners unquestionably have a rich and diverse field from which to choose a course of study. In light of all this I strongly believe that, generally speaking, students should limit themselves to learning and fully developing in just one style only.

Contrary to what is widely believed today, there were few highly regarded kung-fu practitioners in history who studied more than one style. Undertaking the study of too many styles can in fact limit your potential rather than expand it. Kung-fu cannot be treated as an art item to be collected, coveted, and shared with fellow art lovers. Rather, it is a very practical and realistic assortment of techniques constructed for the primary purpose of self-protection.

There were few highly regarded kung-fu practitioners in history who studied more than one style.

At times aspects of other systems could also be introduced, but only for the purpose of supplementing the overall kung-fu training. This type of learning situation depends mostly on an individual student's characteristics and need not necessarily be applied to everyone. I still consider this approach as practicing just one style.

As previously mentioned, learning too many systems can indeed do more harm than good. Some training methods unique to particular kung-fu styles can in fact be counterproductive, pulling the student in opposite directions.

The goal of serious kung-fu students is to fully develop their potential, and through systematic and unrelenting commitment they should become one with their style. Each and every movement and gesture should carry a characteristic flavor and personality. Pursuing different styles will impede one's ability to thoroughly internalize and purify the techniques of a chosen style.

An old Chinese saying cautions that "to learn too much is like owing money." The opening line of the Confucian *Analects* advises us to "learn and practice often." By learning many styles and collecting forms, we simply cannot have sufficient time to practice. Naturally, as is true with any discipline, improvement and proper understanding without practice is impossible. In olden times one's life depended on mastery of techniques; the margin for error was indeed very small. Learning both the saber and sword, for example, would be impractical, since the qualities of each are so dramatically different that any confusion in technique during battle could result in death. The real kung-fu practitioner could not waste time being a style collector.

> *Pursuing different styles will impede one's ability to thoroughly internalize and purify the techniques of a chosen style.*

During those times there were also limits as to just how much one person could actually learn. The real techniques were not easily given away and passed down from instructor to student; only a few family members and loyal students were given the treasures. To find an instructor willing to teach the entire style was difficult enough; to completely learn and utilize more than one, nearly impossible. Various styles were also traditionally bitter enemies. If a student admitted studying with an opposing teacher, he would be treated as a spy and either turned away or purposely misled.

Martial arts novels and movies have contributed greatly to the myth that the ideal martial arts man should be expert in any number and variety of styles and weapons. For example, the saying, "Of 18 different weapons, all can be expertly used," is taken from these romanticized heroic tales which have been mistakenly ascribed as a valuable kung-fu teaching. This is ridiculous. No one can handle 18 kinds of weapons effectively. We have created new sayings, born from these wrong ideas to help express the correct concepts: "If you learn 18 weapons, then every one will be lousy."

Staying with a single style is really not so unusual. Looking at the Japanese martial arts, we see that most *judoka* do not punch and kick powerfully like *karateka;* most *karateka* can't handle the sword as proficiently as the *kendoka*. We cannot possibly say that their training is incomplete; on the contrary by correctly remaining within each chosen discipline, they are assured that their art will survive and perhaps last forever.

In modern times, teaching has became more open and people have the opportunity to learn many different styles. Unfortunately, due to personal shortcomings and an inability to raise their techniques to a higher level, people cheat themselves by collecting various forms. Quantity becomes a very poor substitute for quality. Up to and including today, most people feel that the more they learn, the more qualified they have become.

I have much more respect for a single-style practitioner, and therefore exercise more care when matching against such a person. Fighting a person who knows many styles does not interest me. In fact, someone who collects styles is easier to confuse and defeat.

I often point to myself as an example to my students of someone who has had the misfortune of having learned too many styles. I was always searching for a good kung-fu system that would best suit my own psychological and physical make-up. Perhaps even worse, during these years I found many systems that I still thought valuable and wished to do my best to help develop and spread, even though they may not have fit me that well. I had to partially sacrifice my time, energy, and overall potential for the continued development of kung-fu as a whole.

All of my students major in a single style in which they will hopefully complete the entire training.

Today, I continue to teach a much greater variety of styles than I really want to or should. In this country there are not yet enough qualified instructors, so I feel compelled to teach multiple styles as a way of ensuring their future.

All of my students major in a single style in which they will hopefully complete the entire training. In individual cases I may introduce aspects of other styles to help, just as a doctor will prescribe medicine to cure a sickness. Once the sickness is gone, it is no longer required that the patient continue taking the medication. It is not necessary for the student to complete these other helping styles once the prescription has cured the disease.

In this modern society we have a great many responsibilities, pressure, and diversions that make it extremely difficult to devote ourselves fully to the practice and mastery of kung-fu. As kung-fu means time and skill, it is essential that we use what time we do have intelligently to practice seriously, honestly, and in depth, rather than collecting forms and never progressing beyond a superficial level.

If kung-fu is to survive and hopefully grow and improve, then we must have experts who thoroughly understand their styles, and are qualified to pass them on. This goal can be most realistically achieved by selecting the style most suitable and making it a lifelong commitment.

Piecing Together the Kung-fu Puzzle

An old kung-fu saying states: "One hundred techniques you know cannot compare with one technique you have mastered."

If I feel so strongly about dedication to a single style, then why have I learned so many different systems? Perhaps, unknowingly, I have misled the kung-fu public.

To clear the air, a tour of my training history is in order. I was fortunate to find many great *sifus* (teachers) who were willing to share their art. I began by studying with Sifu Han Ching Tang, an instructor who taught me not only the jai men (Islamic) and mei hua (plum blossom) systems of changquan (long fist), but also a variety of weapons and two-person forms. The energy I spent practicing changquan gave me a good foundation for the future.

I always treated kung-fu primarily as a martial art, not just as an exercise or performing art. I had to be able to use it in real fighting to give myself confidence. Initially, when sparring with my changquan classmates, I discovered the techniques differed only slightly from our "natural" way of fighting. To improve, I had to fight faster, stronger, and more fearlessly. There were times when I would beat even my senior classmate, who was stronger and more experienced. Then I would lose to a beginner who had just been taught the horse stance.

This situation was difficult to accept. I could do forms beautifully and skillfully, but I couldn't use my changquan. At the time, I lacked the maturity to realize changquan is a formidable and highly sophisticated kung-fu fighting system.

The deficiency I felt triggered a desire to seek out other styles, such as tanglang (praying mantis) kung-fu, which is famous for its rapid and complex succession of techniques. I was lucky enough to first study the eight-step tanglang style (which combined techniques from other styles like tongbeiquan and xingyiquan) from Sifu Wei Hsiao Tang. Then I studied the chi xing (seven-stars) tanglang style under Sifu Li Kung Shan, the dean of chi xingyi instructors.

Like most tanglangquan practitioners, I felt I could use my kung-fu in actual fighting situations. But I also was able to apply it to changquan techniques I never before understood. The tanglang style made me more conscious when I was fighting, and I suddenly knew why I would win or lose a bout.

Although my sparring ability improved, I realized I could not generate the power to inflict enough damage once contact was made. In kung-fu, the practitioner trains to destroy the target. Anything less and you encourage your opponent to come back for more.

At this stage of my kung-fu career, I thought all I needed was a more effective way of delivering power, and after some searching, began my training in xingyiquan with Sifu Chao Lien Fang, who soon would request my discipleship. This presented quite a problem, not so much because I favored one style over another, but because this traditional method of training failed to promote kung-fu in our contemporary society. Although a product of that traditional style, I sensed that reverting to the old fashioned way would only help bring a quicker end to kung-fu.

After receiving his M.A. in Chinese literature, the author revisited his first kung-fu teacher, Sifu Han Ching Tan.

Despite our differences, Sifu Chao gave me years to make my decision. I still thank him for not only leading me into xingyi, but also helping me to meet Sifu Liu Yun Chiao, my last instructor.

Sifu Liu had the opportunity to study a variety of northern Chinese kung-fu styles with the most accomplished teachers of his time. He never insisted I quit all the previous styles, just that I forget everything I ever learned!

Because I was still searching for power, I thought the forceful style of bajiquan would be the first system I learned. Based on my extensive experience, opening with baji would signal an immediate desire for more power and strength. I certainly could have learned baji, but my style would have become a watered-down version of all the previous styles. Instead, I began with piquazhang, which forced me to start from scratch. Only then could I develop the correct way to use power.

Stretching exercises helped me relax and improve my flexibility, keys to restructuring myself in the piqua way. Becoming a beginner all over again was one of the most painful things I've ever had to do. The pain, I believe, is why many people can't learn kung-fu. They are unwilling to let go, choosing to shy away from pain at the expense of their potential.

Eventually, I learned how to issue power through baji/piqua training with Sifu Liu. This type of practice is endless, mirroring the old saying, "There is always another mountain that is higher."

Although satisfied with baji/piqua training, I found myself studying even more styles. Since the end of the Qing dynasty (1644–1912), the true kung-fu practitioners discovered their beloved martial arts were less important to the social order. Shocked and heartbroken, they lost their sense of worth. The need to teach kung-fu to the next generation lessened dramatically.

With the traditional kung-fu facing potential extinction, Sifu Liu wanted me to shoulder some of the responsibility for preserving this priceless jewel. He also introduced me to his good friends: Sifu Chang Hsiang Shan, who taught me liouhe (six harmonies) tanglang, and Sifu Tu Yi Che, who schooled me in the original Chen-style taijiquan. In Sifu Chang's 30 years of teaching, I was his first liouhe student. Sifu Tu learned the Chen style from Sifu Chen Yen Hsi, father of famous instructor Sifu Chen Fa Ke.

At the outset of my training with Sifu Liu, I never realized the true meaning and responsibility contained within the art's scripture. Sifu Liu's genuine concern for preserving kung-fu gradually became my own. Today, it remains one of my most precious goals.

Sifu Liu Yun Chiao's genuine concern for preserving kung-fu gradually became my own.

My kung-fu training was long and filled with obstacles. I sought out many different styles, not because I thought more was better, but because of basic needs that had to be fulfilled. Putting the kung-fu puzzle together wasted needless time and energy-time that would have been better spent developing and maturing in a single style.

Any complete kung-fu system taught by a qualified instructor should contain the necessary aspects of training: technique, usage, and power. Using my own experiences as a backdrop, I hope to spare aspiring students some of the confusion and frustration inherent in learning kung-fu. In the end, barriers, distractions, and difficulties should be easier to sidestep.

I currently teach several kung-fu styles, and believe it is important to pass them down to my students. Some of these styles are new to America and are known by only a few instructors. In addition, I have come to know many other styles quite well, including styles from a variety of China's provinces.

Counterfeit Kung-fu

When I was still living in Taiwan, I sometimes heard about or met people who had created their own styles in places such as Hong Kong, Macao, Singapore, and Malaysia. Each claimed his "new style" was based on kung-fu. I was always skeptical of their claims, but I would try to give them the benefit of the doubt. Perhaps I didn't know them well enough or possibly they hid their good kung-fu from me. None of the kung-fu stylists had significant real fighting experience, however, and some were just delinquents who had learned what little they knew on the street.

If we compare these examples with the circumstances in which the traditional styles were created, we can see the absurdity of it all. In ancient times, a practitioner attempting to create a style would have already mastered at least one existing style. The founder of the new style may have combined several different complete styles to create what he thought to be a more balanced system, such as baji/piqua. In the case of Choy Lay Fut, the founders took only the best techniques from various styles.

Typically, a new system reflects and leverages the founder's particular body size or strength.

Typically, a new system reflects and leverages the founder's particular body size or strength, such as the long-armed baguazhang, or Wing Chun, a style created by a woman.

Regardless of the style, its true worth was proven on the battlefield. Any practitioner proclaiming a new style was subjected to a testing period during which challenges were issued. If the style and, more importantly, the practitioner could stand up to the challenges, a new style was established. If it failed to vanquish the challengers, the new style was discarded.

Today, this kind of testing would be too dangerous. Consequently, anyone can claim to have created a new style. Unfortunately, these alleged new styles are often unreliable and can't be trusted.

The new styles introduced into the United States typically fall into three categories. First is the established style that merely gains a new name. Sometimes the name is changed because the country where the style originated is despised by the country from which it was adopted. Nations don't easily forget their conquerors, and crediting them with an acquired martial art damages their self-respect.

Business is another reason for changing a style's name. The promoters find their product easier to advertise as a new style, or they might want to remove the restrictions of being affiliated with a larger organization.

Second is the new style that doesn't have a home of its own. Try establishing the style's origin, and you'll find no one in a particular country ever heard of it. Did it come from someone studying martial arts books or movies, or from watching other schools? Practitioners of this new style sometimes have martial art training, but are usually of a low rank in an authentic style. However, they

The author checking out the weapons at the 108 Heroes Conference Hall in Liang Shan, Shandong province, China.

will name an exalted leader of their new style and boast of the major tournaments won by the founder. If you were to check on the roots of the style, you would likely find that the leader had died and the style is untraceable.

Finally, we have the new style that some claim mixes kung-fu and some other martial arts. Sometimes it is even called a kind of kung-fu. The proponents emphasize the kung-fu components, or claim that their new style is an improvement on authentic kung-fu because it can be used in real fighting situations.

I believe that every country has native martial arts. In Asia, China was the martial leader for thousands of years. Many neighboring countries were influenced by or attempted to mix kung-fu into their native styles. Over time, some of these countries successfully developed their martial art and spread it throughout the world.

Kung-fu has been susceptible to counterfeiting because it has proven difficult to promote and organize.

Martial art is not merely fighting technique but also a kind of reflection of the society it represents. Every country should be credited with the growth and shaping of its martial art.

Kung-fu has been susceptible to counterfeit styles because it has proven difficult to promote and organize committees to establish standards. In ancient times, the Chinese never taught real kung-fu to neighboring countries. To teach the secret kung-fu to foreigners would have been like the United States teaching the Russians how to make the MX missile.

Some say that as late as the late 19th- or early 20th-century, kung-fu was learned from the Chinese, as in the case of some Okinawan martial artists. During that period in history, even the Chinese thought kung-fu was useless. They had been beaten by the guns of the foreigners. It was not an ideal time to learn kung-fu from the Chinese. If individuals, through some good fortune, learned real kung-fu, reached a high level, and brought it back to their own countries, I haven't seen it.

The easiest way to identify kung-fu is to look at the way a style is used. Practitioners of these new styles often claim they can use kung-fu to fight. I have seen these practitioners fight in tournaments and perform in demonstrations. I have also read their books and articles explaining their style's usage. It is not kung-fu.

The kung-fu way to fight is very distinct and identifiable. It is a way of fighting that I teach in my classes and workshops. It involves principles such as the "door" (the divisions of and the space around the body used to analyze the relationship between combatants), the use of the whole arm and body, multiple attacking and defending techniques, and the development of pure kung-fu power. The practitioners I've referred to may be good in their own area; that's not for me to judge. However, if you're talking about kung-fu, they have yet to step in the door.

Part 4

The Role of Forms
in Kung-fu

Is It Necessary to Learn Forms?

In the late 1970s, when I first began teaching kung-fu in the United States, the first training I gave my students was forms. A few years later when I restarted these students with basic and single-movement training, I was surprised and encouraged to find that they were not angered or disappointed. On the contrary, they were grateful.

Single-movement training improves the student's body condition and also begins to impart the unique flavor of the style.

By that time they felt they were having great difficulty in improving their forms. They understood that the seemingly boring basic training was essential to their improvement. Subsequently almost all the students asked the same logical question: "Why weren't we taught basics before the forms?" I explained that if I had started them with the tedious, repetitive basic training, they would have stopped their training. They would have thought I had nothing to teach. Unfortunately, most people believe kung-fu consists only of the beautiful combined movements in forms.

The point I want to make clear is that kung-fu has a step-by-step, complete training system, of which forms are a part. In sports, dance, or martial arts, everyone should start with basics, and kung-fu is no exception.

I would like to explain the traditional kung-fu training procedure by using our contemporary educational system as a guideline. Students begin with basic training—punching, kicking, static postures, and fundamental movements. This is elementary school. After students qualify in the basics, the instructor teaches single-movement training. These are, in fact, the movements and techniques of which forms are comprised. Single-movement training improves the student's body condition and also begins to impart the unique flavor of the style. In addition, the instructor begins to teach usage. When students have achieved some proficiency in single-movement training, it can be said that they have earned a high school diploma.

College is the next level in the kung-fu education. In addition to continual practice of basics, the college level emphasizes two-person training. Students apply the usage training that began at the high school level. All the repetitive practice has strengthened the students and taught them a new way of moving. They learn to link the single movements, at first in a predetermined way, and later spontaneously and creatively. In learning these skills, the students have earned a college degree.

Not everyone needs a Ph.D., but some desire to further pursue their kung-fu education. Students who are seriously interested in an advanced degree must be willing to research their art. They must have the potential to reach the high level and find a qualified instructor to accept them. If students meet these requirements, they can continue training in their style at the Doctoral level. At this level, students polish their skills, adding more basics, single-movement, and usage training.

Forms can enhance the student's fluidity of movement, especially transitions from one movement to another.

In addition, form training is essential.

We can see now that forms are traditionally taught at the high-level stages of training. You may ask why forms are traditionally taught at the advanced level rather than at the beginning as we are accustomed to seeing. Technically speaking, the answer is that single movements are easier to perfect than combinations of movements. Moreover, in relation to usage, forms can enhance the student's fluidity of movement, especially transitions from one movement to another.

One of the most difficult skills in kung-fu is the ability to change movements. This skill is a primary aspect of forms. When you are able to swiftly and smoothly change movements, your chances of defeating an opponent are greatly increased.

It is important to see form training within the context of a larger system. All of the training, from basic stances to freestyle fighting, is interrelated and necessary. It is a sequence of overlapping steps. Forms are a variety of connected movements with challenging transitions. These two parts of training—single movements and forms—are compatible tools of practice, each adding depth to the other.

> Students learn to use their qi throughout the form, accenting specific movements and issuing power.

Forms also effectively establish one's ability to create and alter rhythm and tempo. This heightens both physical and psychological flexibility, making one an elusive and confusing foe for an opponent.

Another side to form training is learning to manage the *qi* (energy). Students learn to use their *qi* throughout the form, accenting specific movements and issuing power. Long forms have been developed especially for *qi* training.

Forms are also the fundamental way by which the flavor of a particular style is shown. Any expression of art, at its highest level, is identifiable by its unique flavor. The works of great composers, painters, or filmmakers are recognizable by a distinctive flavor. Good kung-fu also transmits this quality.

It should be clear now that forms are an important and necessary element of a complete kung-fu education. Forms are not a prerequisite for fighting. They can be employed at the undergraduate level, but it is not necessary. Anyone graduating from a genuine kung-fu college can fight without forms.

Some instructors believe that forms can interfere with one's ability to fight. If this is so, we must look to ancient times for the reasons. In the past, instructors often hid their real techniques and instead taught beautiful forms. Whereas single-movement training shows each movement clearly and completely, forms can often conceal the real usage.

During the Ming dynasty (1368–1644), the famous General Che Chi Kwong noted that forms were overemphasized. Nowadays, it is commonly thought that if people know many forms, they have good kung-fu. We should not confuse quantity with quality. Students who spend their time learning multitudes of forms are wasting their time. This kind of practice, void of a true foundation, is no more than folk dance. Traditionally, good kung-fu systems, such as taijiquan, mizongquan, piquazhang, baguazhang, and bajiquan, have three to five forms. Each form has its own purpose and each form is one step in a clear progression of training.

For students with a correct kung-fu education, form training is like the watchmaker in the final stages of his labor. Each of his finely tooled parts, products of serious and exacting work, are at last united as a single, functional unit. The kung-fu form itself can be appreciated for its practicality as well as its beauty, for its subtlety as well as its elegance. When practiced by a highly proficient student, the form projects power, confidence, and a seeming effortlessness that belies the fact it is built upon the repetitive and disciplined work of basic training.

Form Without Content

The process of learning kung-fu, or other arts such as painting or ballet, is fraught with difficulty and potential pitfalls. Essentially, the instructor's role is to guide students through the training, helping them to avoid those pitfalls. One of the more common problems is students indiscriminately imitating the instructor's movements. Just as budding artists mimic the techniques of masters like DaVinci or Picasso, fledgling kung-fu practitioners mimic their instructor's elegant, powerful movements.

Mimicking is human nature—that's how children learn. However, a huge gap exists between the instructor's level and that of the student. When novice students watch the instructor's movements and then copy them, they can only produce a weak imitation of the original. It's like creating a Picasso painting with a paint-by-numbers kit—you can only produce a superficial imitation of the classic work. Even worse, students who habitually mimic their instructor's movements can kill their potential to reach a high level of expertise.

> *The gap between the student and the instructor cannot be bridged without going through the step-by-step training process.*

The gap between the student and the instructor cannot be bridged without going through the step-by-step training process. You cannot hide from sweat, pain, or the labor of arduous training. There are no shortcuts. If you skip steps in the training process, you will have form minus the content. When you get into a real fighting situation, your lack of sufficient training will be painfully revealed. Students must realize that just as Rome was not built in a day, becoming a kung-fu instructor requires years of dedicated practice.

Instructors must be aware of the needs and abilities of their students. If an instructor is giving a workshop, it is a good chance

to learn something. I've often introduced my students in Taiwan, Japan, and the United States to other instructors for such occasions. In this short period, however, the information students can absorb is limited. They can quickly become confused if the instructor doesn't consider their level when he or she is teaching.

In one instance, a noted instructor told several of my beginning students the horse stance is double-weighted (the

The author holds bajiquan horse stance in Meng Village, a strong-hold of the style.

weight is equally distributed on both legs). Hence it is impractical for usage. My students then wondered why they spent so much time practicing the horse stance. Essentially, the instructor's advice was correct, but he didn't take into account the level of the students. The instructor's action in this case is comparable to the famous doctor who prescribes 500 milligrams instead of 50 milligrams of medicine for the patient. The overdose can adversely affect the student's progress.

In terms of practical usage, of course, you don't want to be double weighted. The differences between training and usage, however, may not be clear to beginning students. Check any kung-fu style and you will find that the horse stance is an essential part of the basic training. Practicing the horse stance builds a strong foundation, helping students to increase leg strength and improve balance. The horse stance, like a middle C note in a musical scale, also serves as the standard or home base; you can fluidly change from the horse stance to any other stance.

In my own class, I divide the training into different levels. This arrangement gives students a clear idea of where they are in the training process and what they have to do to improve. The famous changquan (long fist) forms, for example, are divided into three levels. While the forms don't change within each level, the way to perform them differs.

In the first level, movements are done one-by-one, while making sure each technique is performed correctly. Some postures can be held for a number of breaths to help build the students' foundations. During this stage, students should not be concerned with performing the movements fast or with a lot of power.

The second level adds advancing and retreating steps to the techniques, giving students a better idea of how to apply the step in usage. Students learn how to adjust the distance, timing, and angle according to the demands of the situation. Step training also helps students improve their leg stability.

Students are required to develop their own tempo and rhythm, blending the form with their own character.

When students reach the third level, their legs are stronger and long fist forms can be done smoothly and accurately. This capability allows them to gain more control over the movements and capture the distinctive flavor of the style. At this stage, the kung-fu practitioner is like the artist who has spent years carefully studying the techniques of the masters and is now ready to create his or her own masterpiece. Students are required to develop their own tempo and rhythm, blending the form with their own character. Thus, each practitioner's rendering of the form will be somewhat different.

Some students are too clever and try to practice the higher level before they are ready. If their foundation is not strong enough to perform second-level step training, for example, students may compensate by executing the techniques incorrectly, which can destroy their potential.

Students from the author's Taiwan school practice amid the beautiful columns of the Chiang Kai-Sheck Memorial Hall in Taipei.

Obviously, kung-fu cannot benefit from an environment that inhibits students from developing the correct skills. I encourage all instructors to set up clearly defined training levels. The requirements of different levels can then be used as a means of qualifying students for promotion. This way we can insure the authentic kung-fu tradition will be preserved and each student will at least have a chance to become a martial artist, and not just an imitator.

Analyze Your Beauty

Many people would agree that among the martial arts kung-fu has the most beautiful movements. Hidden within those graceful movements, however, is a potential danger. Many practitioners get lost in the beautiful forms. They get off the track of the real kung-fu, chasing fancy, acrobatic movements like circus performers. Training that way eventually reduces the quality of kung-fu because practitioners lose contact with techniques and usage that make kung-fu an effective fighting art.

This problem is most apparent in the new modern kung-fu developed by the mainland Chinese government. They use the term wushu, literally defined as "martial art" but literally meaning "fighting technique," to describe their art. The emphasis is purely on performance, however. Movements from modern wushu are mixed with ballet, Western floor gymnastics, and elements of Chinese acrobatics and Peking opera. In addition, the authentic fighting techniques are modified with the intention of making them more beautiful and graceful. Wushu is certainly enjoyable to watch, but this modern fusion of movement arts and kung-fu, including the two-person and multiple-person fighting forms, is completely useless for fighting.

Wushu is certainly enjoyable to watch, but this modern fusion of movement arts and kung-fu . . . is completely useless for fighting.

Just as kung-fu movies caught peoples' imaginations some years ago and came to represent kung-fu in the public eye, wushu now symbolizes China's ancient tradition of kung-fu to the world.

Millions of people in China and throughout the world practice modern wushu. This is an unfortunate situation for kung-fu because very little real martial art exists in the wushu training or forms.

Most people, including the majority of kung-fu practitioners, cannot distinguish the differences between real and phony kung-fu. Some may be shocked, surprised, even horrified by my remarks about modern wushu. While I'm not strong enough to argue with the millions of wushu lovers who contend that it represents China's authentic martial art, I believe the traditional kung-fu can speak for itself. Practitioners just need to take time to analyze their forms, regardless of style, in light of a few basic principles.

A kung-fu form, no matter how flowery or fancy, consists of specific, identifiable components. These fundamental components serve a variety of purposes such as physical conditioning and training in basics, usage, and power issuance. Physical conditioning, for example, includes stretching techniques that are potentially useful for forms that have high kicks or wide stances. In practical usage, kicks are usually low and stances smaller, but

If you execute the movements correctly, showing the correct usage, power, flavor, tempo, and spirit, there will be a natural beauty to your forms.

some movements are designed in part to help practitioners loosen up. Balance is another basic physical requirement in kung-fu. Standing on one leg, jumping in the air, and twisting movements all help to improve balance.

Coordinating body movements is also an important aspect of physical conditioning. Each technique requires that you orchestrate different parts of the body to achieve a specific goal. When you throw a straight punch for example, the legs, waist, back, shoulders, arms, as well as the fist must coordinate to deliver the blow.

Some movements in a form may appear unnecessary—such as striking with one arm as the other does a small, seemingly insignificant movement—but the overall purpose is to force you to use your whole body to perform the technique.

Another fundamental component in kung-fu forms is basic training. This shows up in repeated movements such as a straight punch that occurs several times throughout the form. Holding postures, such as the horse stance, also helps build a basic foundation, as does practicing different kinds of steps for approaching and retreating.

In beginning level forms, the movements often emphasize physical conditioning and basic training. As the student's fundamentals improve, the major component of form training should focus on developing practical usage. Some techniques are primarily defensive, while others are offensive. Even more effective are techniques that combine both offense and defense in one movement. Another element of usage training provided by forms is linking a series of continuous movements. In any case, a form filled with fancy, impractical movements is like a book with a beautifully decorated cover but lacks useful content within its pages.

The ability to execute techniques correctly must be combined with the power to damage an opponent.

The ability to execute techniques correctly must be combined with the power to damage an opponent. The power training component in forms varies depending on the style. Some styles emphasize the upper extremities, focusing on the fist, elbow, shoulder, or even head to issue power. Other styles might emphasize the lower extremities or a combination of upper and lower to issue power. Also, some types of power are more visible than others. This doesn't mean that baguazhang, in which the power is somewhat hidden, is less powerful than bajiquan, in which the power is easy to see.

Among the other training components developed in forms is the unique flavor of a style. A classically trained ballerina, for example, wouldn't want to mix her techniques with those of a gymnast. Similarly, mixing kung-fu with other movement arts or even with other kung-fu styles pollutes the special flavor and techniques of the art. The forms of some styles such as xingyiquan are characterized by a fairly regular tempo. In others, like mizongquan, the tempo can change dramatically in series of movements. Spirit training is incorporated into forms as well. Sometimes the head is raised or you hold a posture to summon your spirit.

The least important component is beauty. In the past, instructors sometimes tried to hide their real techniques by adopting pretty movements as seen in Chinese paintings and sculpture. That practice was mainly used to prevent outsiders from learning their kung-fu. In reality, beauty has never been a requirement of kung-fu. However, if you execute the movements correctly, showing the correct usage, power, flavor, tempo, and spirit, there will be a natural beauty to your forms. You won't need cosmetics or useless fancy movements to compensate for a lack of proficiency.

If you examine forms based on the components outlined above, you can gain understanding about the differences between modern wushu and real kung-fu. Wushu forms have good conditioning training and basics, but the basics are not designed for martial art. The attacking and defensive movements in wushu forms are mostly ineffective for fighting, and wushu practitioners are not concerned with issuing power. Of course, beautiful movements have become a wushu trademark, and the practitioners display a unique flavor, tempo, and spirit in their forms.

I agree that modern wushu is an entertaining performing art, but to sacrifice the simple beauty and richness of traditional kung-fu for its gymnastic, dramatic beauty is like trading a diamond for a piece of shiny glass. My advice to all kung-fu practitioners is to analyze your forms, and see if you are polishing a diamond or a lump of shiny glass.

Forms and Function

Kung-fu is demanding. It requires the full attention and participation of mind and body. Elements such as patience, perseverance, *yi* (mind intent), strength, flexibility, and *qi* are essential in developing one's kung-fu skills.

Another less obvious element seems to be lacking in many people's practice, however. Many practitioners don't have a clear idea of what they are trying to achieve.

Perhaps you've met a practitioner who is really kung-fu crazy. He has studied many kung-fu styles over 10 or 20 years, following half a dozen instructors in a quest to become an expert. Kung-fu is deeply rooted in his life. He practices several hours a day, has a large collection of kung-fu books and magazines, weapons and training equipment. Perhaps he even knows how to speak or read Chinese. He knows 50 to 100 different forms and 25 ways to counterattack a side kick. He attends and performs at various kung-fu demonstrations, helps his instructor teach, or even has his own school.

A common misconception is that the more philosophy, forms, and techniques you know, the better your kung-fu.

On the surface, this person would appear to be proficient in kung-fu. But when you probe further, you find a crucial element is missing. For all his years of training and collection of kung-fu knowledge, he cannot actually demonstrate what he knows. He cannot convert his vast knowledge into practical application. Given that fighting is the bottom line of kung-fu, this is a serious problem.

Students hold the Chen taijiquan old form's "single whip" posture.

In learning kung-fu, students should try to maintain a clear understanding of what they are doing, making sure their daily practice is focused on the correct principles. It is not enough to know how to deliver a straight punch—you must be able to do it. A helpful way to guide yourself along this difficult path is to learn kung-fu in terms of three basic, interrelated categories: knowledge, ability, and experience.

Knowledge includes philosophy, theory, principle, and history pertinent to kung-fu, as well as basic training techniques and forms. A common misconception is that the more philosophy, forms, and techniques you know, the better your kung-fu.

Some instructors teach dozens of forms and techniques, certain that they possess the real treasures of kung-fu. The various forms they practice appear to be different, but all have the same taste. It's as if you ordered a ten-course dinner at a restaurant known for its fine cuisine, but all the dishes tasted the same. Theoretically, a set of kung-fu forms or techniques should represent a sequence of different training levels, each technique building on the foundation of the previous one.

Knowledge is certainly important, but if you don't go beyond accumulating forms, techniques, and styles, it means nothing as a martial art. It's like a person who knows everything about swimming but has never been in the water.

More important than the breadth of knowledge you have is the ability to demonstrate what you know. A practitioner who learns only a few forms and techniques, but has the ability to make practical use of his knowledge, is certainly better off than the student who learns fifty forms but cannot implement the correct technique usage. I've often seen practitioners demonstrate a form with seeming grace and beauty, but without a single movement being technically correct. These students obviously didn't understand how to use the techniques that make up the form.

> A practitioner who learns only a few forms and techniques, but has the ability to make practical use of his knowledge, is certainly better off than the student who learns fifty forms but cannot implement the correct technique usage.

To avoid this facade, you should compare what you know to what you can physically perform. Ask yourself if your movements have adequate speed and power, or show a certain flavor and tempo. And most importantly, ask yourself if you can perform the techniques correctly without thinking. If you cannot answer yes to those questions, you have learned a valuable lesson. Once you begin to see the relationship between knowledge and ability, and spot areas in which you are deficient, you have an opportunity to improve.

At this point, the third category, experience, comes into play. Ultimately, you want the knowledge gained from kung-fu training to become so ingrained that your ability to use the art is instinctive. During a fight, there is no time to check your notes or look in a book to determine the correct action.

Gaining experience in fighting is of course an essential element in kung-fu training. There is no better way to gauge your progress once you reach the sparring stage than to mix it up with an opponent. You can see your strengths and weaknesses, and use that knowledge to correct your deficiencies. Thus, experience enhances one's knowledge and improves overall ability.

Traditional instructors can help students achieve their goals and maintain a high quality of kung-fu by sharing their knowledge and experience. By designing systematic training methods, instructors can help create an atmosphere in which students have a clearer idea of their purpose in studying kung-fu. Rather than collecting forms, students will have a focused framework within which to develop their kung-fu. Eventually, those students will be able to draw on their own knowledge, ability, and experience to help the next generation of kung-fu practitioners reach their goals.

Two-person Forms: Martial or Performing Art?

Defending oneself is the purpose of a martial art. You may learn a famous kung-fu style and many techniques, but you cannot effectively fight without sparring training. All other training methods—warming up, stretching, stances, step training, basic technique, breath training, and two-person forms—are preparation for free sparring.

Kung-fu schools today commonly emphasize two-person forms, such as bare-hand versus bare-hand, bare-hand versus weapon, weapon versus weapon, and one person versus multiple attackers. Most of these prearranged fighting forms can be graceful and exciting, depending on the performer's ability. Sadly, however, forms of this type are becoming more of a performing art and less useful for training in martial art.

In some schools, students are led to believe that by practicing two-person forms they will naturally be able to use their kung-fu in a real fight. This is false. In ancient times, two-person forms had several purposes. One was as a performing art for demonstration at festivals and on holidays.

A second purpose was to give the student

Sanshou (individual movement training) is the proper phase of training to be undertaken before free sparring.

a type of psychological training. The prearranged movements helped to prepare students for free sparring by instilling a bit of courage. Prearranged forms simulate real fighting conditions. When a hand or a spear goes toward the face, one knows enough to at least move the head and not just close the eyes. When a foot sweep or a knife is directed at the leg, one learns to jump up and not freeze with fear.

In ancient times this stage of training was brief because instructors didn't want students to become too comfortable and fearless. After all, in this situation the practitioner knows when a fist or leg will come, and knows that it won't be lethal. In addition, the student who practices prearranged forms for an extended period runs the risk of being conditioned to feel that the enemy is not an opponent but a partner.

When I was younger, my teacher didn't allow me to engage in much two-person training. He said, "Don't envy those who do it beautifully, because it only proves they can't learn martial arts at all. If you do too much training of this kind, your hand becomes too kind, too merciful." Unfortunately, by overemphasizing this aspect of training many instructors, knowingly or unknowingly, are damaging their students.

The third reason two-person forms were practiced in ancient times was that instructors wanted to create an illusion. Rather than reveal what they were determined to keep hidden, the teachers created exciting forms that thrilled audiences but were without much martial value. There is a saying attributed to an ancient instructor: "During the day I don't worry about a thousand people watching me. And even at night my kung-fu can't be stolen."

The prearranged two-person form has its place in kung-fu training as long as it is not overemphasized.

For purposes of advertising entertainment, or just to show off, the instructors did give demonstrations. The forms they illustrated were full of incomplete movements and baffling changes of direction. The actual purpose of the movements was changed from that of practice usage to just being pretty.

In two-person forms, the situation was even worse. In order to confuse their enemies' spies and hide their special techniques, the teachers purposely integrated incorrect usage into the forms. This kind of form only entertained the general audience and cheated the enemy; it was not designed for usage or real training.

The prearranged two-person form has its place in kung-fu training as long as it is not overemphasized. Additionally, moving directly from two-person forms into free sparring is an error. *Sanshou* (individual movement training) is the proper phase of training before free sparring, and should be practiced for a considerable length of time. In *sanshou* practice, students pair off and work through individual offensive and defensive techniques. Later, they practice the techniques in combination.

Initially, all techniques are predetermined. For instance, one student punches to the head and the other blocks, or kicks to the body then punches to the head. At this level of *sanshou,* both opponents know in advance where each strike will be aimed and in what sequence the blows will come.

Later as *sanshou* training progresses with several movements in combination, the sequence and location of the strikes is not wholly predetermined. In this case, the defender will be told, for example, that the head and body will be attacked. However, the sequence of the attack is not established. Also, the exact kind of strike that will be used is not prearranged—a head attack may come in the form of a straight punch or perhaps as a back-fist.

The semi-freestyle sparring of high-level *sanshou* guarantees the purity of the practitioner's offensive and defensive techniques, and paves the way for the spontaneous action of free sparring. Every kung-fu style has its own specialty techniques. To complete his kung-fu training, the practitioner must become proficient with the chosen style's particular techniques in a fighting situation.

Part 5

Mind and Body Training

Starting with a Clean Slate

In any sport, artistic discipline, or work-related function, you must master the unique movements of the particular activity to become proficient. In martial arts, as well as other disciplines, the task of building correct habits is a gradual process. Pianists do not begin their training with a complex Beethoven sonata; they must first learn to read music and play simple scales. Kung-fu students do not begin their training by learning complex, full-power techniques. They must first grasp and control basic body movements as well as develop sufficient strength to perform those techniques.

Slow, soft movements characterize the beginning of any good kung-fu style.

The first training step in any worthwhile kung-fu system is to eliminate old habits. Kung-fu techniques are based on using the body in a unique, highly disciplined way. Building new habits on top of old ones succeeds only in muddling the process. Rather, old habits should be abolished and clear the way for implanting correct techniques.

The key concept for students at this stage is to think less about power and more about technique while still concentrating on absorbing the *qi,* allowing the internal energy to accumulate. Most people naturally try to showcase their strength and speed when practicing a martial art. Genuine kung-fu training asks students to re-educate their bodies. If beginning students rely on previous habits to attain power, they will not be able to reach higher levels.

Several kung-fu styles have become well-known for their emphasis on soft, slow movement training. Among these styles, xingyiquan, baguazhang, and taijiquan are the most popular and considered more sophisticated and difficult to learn. People often comment on the meditative quality of the movements, and over the years these arts have been classified as internal styles.

Slow, soft movements characterize the beginning of any good kung-fu style. Changquan or piquazhang, styles which are not usually thought of as internal, might fit into this category. As students progress and establish a solid new foundation, they can begin incorporating more speed and power into movements. Replacing old habits in this way allows students to develop their kung-fu more naturally. When fighting a skilled opponent, your reactions must be instantaneous and natural, shaped by kung-fu training that helps you unconsciously adapt to any situation.

So-called internal styles such as taijiquan, baguazhang, and xingyiquan have intermediate- to high-level training that is not always soft and slow. Chen-style taijiquan, for example, is well know for both hard-and-fast as well as soft-and-slow movements. At the outset, the movements are mostly slow and soft, but as the student progresses the majority of techniques are hard and fast with an emphasis on power. A high-level practitioner's techniques may appear simple, and power issuing deceptively soft, but this skill level was the result of years of rigorous training.

The author visits Guan county China, home of chaquan, a Muslim longfist style.

Both xingyi and bagua use special training equipment. At first, students shadow kick and punch to develop strength and balance. At the intermediate level, they begin to use a punching bag to improve technique and develop power. The bagua system also includes weight training in which students walk the circle, lifting heavy iron poles and balls to strengthen the arms.

Kung-fu has adapted to modern times. If your goal in studying kung-fu is health related or artistic in origin, the slow, flowing way will suit your needs. However, don't be fooled by those who say that the soft, "internal" movements are superior to the "external" ones. If you only practice the slow method, you will never develop the skills necessary to defend yourself. If you complete the entire training system, however, you have a good chance of realizing the full benefits and goals of the art.

Don't Tickle My Stomach

When I first learned the English words "martial art," I felt very happy because it was so clever and correct to include the word "art" in the term. After all, the basic character of kung-fu is art, and any art form relies on a person's ability to be creative.

When I was a young kung-fu student, I trained under several different instructors. They taught me many styles, each in a different way. All of my teachers had one important practice in common: none of them ever gave me many opportunities to watch them practice. I was probably no different than today's young kung-fu student. I felt disappointed, and I wanted to see more. At times I would try to trick my teachers into showing me their technique. Of course, most of the time I didn't fool my teachers. They remained seated in their chairs, unmoved by my plotting.

> All of my teachers had one important practice in common: none of them ever gave me many opportunities to watch them practice

I have followed their lead now that I am a teacher. I don't demonstrate too often for my students, except when I feel it's absolutely necessary. I will illustrate why with a story about calligraphy.

When young children learn to write, they start with simple, structured characters and then move on to more complex ones. They go from common words to more elaborate terms. When you begin to write, you go through several stages. The first is called *miao hong* in Chinese. The young Chinese student is given a notebook that is filled with squares. Each square contains a simple character written in red, and the student's job is to write over the red character with black ink. This is *miao hong*.

The second stage is tracing. A piece of rice paper is placed on top of another paper with a character on it. The student traces the character on the rice paper, which is so porous that it allows the copy to soak through and cover the original underneath. The student can then compare the copy to the original.

In the final stage, you have one character on a piece of paper and then attempt to copy it on a separate paper. This is how you

Sifu Tu Yi Che during one of his rare taijiquan demonstrations.

learn to write Chinese characters. However, if you want to become a calligrapher, you must go through three more stages. First, copy the art work of a famous master. Second, do research on the historical changes of various characters. In stage three, you create an original, personal style.

The story of Wang Hsi Chih, a famous Chinese calligrapher, illustrates this process perfectly. Wang loved calligraphy, and he practiced it diligently every day. There was a tiny pond by his house where he would wash his brush and ink stone. He was so diligent that the water in the pond turned black from his constant use.

In addition to his obsession with calligraphy, Wang was very fond of geese. He loved to watch them swim, and he imagined that someday he would be able to use his brush in the same graceful, effortless manner that the geese used their webbed feet for swimming. Wang had a favorite goose he kept as a pet, but one day when he saw a couple of pages of fancy calligraphy that belonged to a passing monk, he traded his precious goose so he could own the calligraphy and attempt to copy it.

One night while he slept, Wang dreamed about calligraphy. In his sleep he reached over and began to write on his wife's stomach.

His wife was furious at being awakened in such an annoying manner, so she pushed him away, yelling "Don't tickle my stomach! Everyone has their own body! Go write on yourself!"

Now, in Chinese, the word for body *(ti)* is the same as the word for style. When Wang heard his wife, he thought she was saying "use you own style!" He realized that if he was to become a great artist, he had to create his own style. He did, and so should you.

Today, I am grateful that my instructors taught me in a traditional way. Even those who treated me cruelly, who seemed to care nothing about my feelings, and who seemed to pay no attention to me, taught me the same lesson: to think for myself. They forced me to practice and make mistakes by myself. If my teachers always practiced alongside me, how could they see my errors or correct my mistakes? They had ample time to watch me. (I needed watching, because I made a lot of mistakes.) When I reached a certain point and really needed my teachers' help, they were always there.

This was an important lesson for me, and one that I am committed to pass on to my students.

Learning to See

Training a new generation of practitioners to preserve and promote traditional kung-fu is an important goal in my life. While I lived in China, I taught kung-fu in the physical education departments of several universities, as well as privately. During more than 15 years of teaching kung-fu in China, I designed training methods that helped students to improve more quickly and grasp the essentials of the art. In 1978 I came to America, looking forward to sharing my kung-fu with Westerners.

After giving a few classes in San Francisco, I realized that teaching Westerners kung-fu was not the same as teaching the Chinese. Westerners have a different body type, cultural heritage, diet, character, and way of thinking than the Chinese. Since that realization, I have struggled to understand the needs of Western students and to develop training methods that make kung-fu more accessible to non-Chinese people.

Encouraging students to learn more about Chinese culture has been helpful. By attending the Chinese opera, studying concepts of Chinese philosophy (such as the theory of *yin* and *yang*), and even learning the Chinese language, students can better savor the unique flavor of China's martial arts and apply that knowledge to their practice.

Some of the cultural differences, however, cannot be resolved simply by absorbing aspects of Chinese culture or modifying training methods. The traditional learning environment for kung-fu can be difficult to handle psychologically. During the first months of training, students may get frustrated because the training is difficult and often painful or boring. They might feel discouraged or unhappy because no one is telling them how great they are or giving them a gold star for their efforts. This type of feedback, which is a typical part of the modern educational process, is not suited to the kung-fu learning environment. Instructors need to encourage students, but not give them false impressions or expectations.

Although kung-fu is a no longer used on the battlefield, the training should prepare students to face a dangerous situation.

A proper learning attitude helps students develop inner strength or character, better powers of concentration, and genuine self-confidence.

Thus, the instructor should act more like a Marine drill sergeant rather than a Boy Scout activities director. The instructor should never try to amuse the student or create a light-hearted atmosphere in class. Students must understand the teacher's duty to create the proper training atmosphere, and they should have a serious attitude, free of expectations of external rewards.

People can argue that because kung-fu is less relevant as a means of self-defense today, such a serious attitude toward training isn't necessary. For serious practitioners, however, an atmosphere in which everyone is obviously enjoying themselves—talking, laughing, or listening to music—can only pollute kung-fu. The soul of kung-fu is its usage, and a serious atmosphere is required if students are to reach a high level. In addition, a proper learning attitude helps students develop inner strength or character, better powers of concentration, and genuine self-confidence.

Another problem I've found is that students often neglect fully using the mind in learning kung-fu. This learning disability can easily show up without the student being aware of it. For example, the instructor may demonstrate a movement and, initially, the student tries to perform the technique correctly. But after a few days, the student unknowingly modifies the technique so that it is grossly incorrect.

I cannot count the number of times I have seen an instructor demonstrate a movement to his students, and the students didn't even watch. They tried to follow along during the demonstration. How can they see what the teacher is doing? How can they pick up the details if they are following, not watching and thinking? Students should not become accustomed to having answers given to them. They are learning to mimic rather than create.

I cannot count the number of times I have seen an instructor demonstrate a movement to his students, and the students didn't even watch.

If my school did nothing but turn out students whose kung-fu looked just like mine, could you call this style a martial art? No. It would only be the cheapest of consumer goods.

To help solve this learning problem, I advise students to use their minds like a videotape recorder. During my training in China, my instructors rarely demonstrated techniques or forms. On the rare occasions when they would demonstrate for me, I learned to watch their movements very carefully. This kind of training later helped me in actual fighting because I could watch my opponent's movement, memorize it, and be ready to counterattack. Years later, I can still replay those images and capture the instructors technique, flavor, and spirit without any fancy electronic equipment. Learning to focus your mind like a camera not only benefits your kung-fu practice, but enhances any kind of study.

I recommend that when the instructor is teaching, students fold their arms together or clasp their hands behind their backs so they are not distracted or tempted to mimic the teacher while he demonstrates a movement. This simple technique helps students to focus on watching the instructor, and recording an accurate image of the movement. At first, students can capture only a single movement, but gradually they'll be able to accurately record two or even three movements at a time.

Obviously, kung-fu is not a purely mental activity like chess. No amount of mental prowess can replace daily practice. From the very beginning throughout the highest training levels, students are instructed to use their minds when they practice. Without applying their minds, students cannot significantly improve their level, no matter how many hours a day they train.

As students reach higher levels of training, they are judged not only by their technical skill and fighting ability, but also by the richness of their movements—the art of martial art that comes from coordinating the mind (internal training) and body (external training). That quality differentiates kung-fu from other athletic endeavors. By adopting the proper learning attitude and using the mind, students are taking an important step toward reaching the highest levels of the art.

Find Your Balance

How often do kung-fu instructors tell students "watch your balance," "relax," or "be calm"? This type of advice is given continually, and no student is exempt from these admonitions. Needless to say, qualities such as balance and relaxation are extremely important in kung-fu training.

These terms are familiar to us, but take on more complex meanings in the realm of kung-fu. Take the word balance, for example. Most people think if they can stand, walk, run, jump, or turn without falling, they have balance. If they have proficiency in some physical activity such as ballet, basketball, or fencing, they assume their balance is even further developed.

Certainly, people who can stand on one toe and kick the other leg overhead while gracefully waving their arms display excellent balance. Furthermore, people who practice a given sport or art develop a characteristic way of using the body particular to the activity. For instance, if a great ballerina competed in the floor exercise event at a gymnastics tournament, most observers would find something odd or unfulfilling about the perfor-

In both kung-fu and Chinese philosophy, balance is synonymous with harmony.

mance. Even though all movements were performed properly, the gymnast's extensive ballet training would show through and the floor exercise would lack the proper gymnastic flavor.

In kung-fu, a person who can execute a dozen consecutive tornado kicks six feet in the air obviously has good balance. Some might think even perfect balance. However, the concept of balance in kung-fu involves much more than the ability to perform tornado kicks. Balance also refers to the relationship between *yin* and *yang*.

In discussing *yin* and *yang* balance, consider movements in which one arm moves away from the body (*yang* movement) while the other arm moves toward the body (*yin* movement). The taijiquan movement "white crane spreads its wings" is a good illustration. Students often technically perform this movement correctly, but when their movement is compared to the instructor's, something is lacking. The missing ingredient is a proper balance of *yin* and *yang*. Usually, students overemphasize the *yang* movement.

The ideal kung-fu movement is neither black nor white. A balanced color, such as gray, is a more accurate description.

The taijiquan movement "single whip" can be used to illustrate internal and external balance. The external movement is obvious: both arms move, the weight shifts forward, and the head turns. The internal movement is harder to describe, but it also must possess its own intrinsic balance. In "single whip," though the head and eyes gaze forward, the mind should not be fixed in a single direction. Instead, you should imagine having another set of eyes in the back of your head that balances your frontal vision. Again, students often perform this movement in a way that is technically correct, but they focus excessively in the forward direction.

The ideal kung-fu movement is neither black nor white. A balanced color such as gray is a more accurate description. In other words, attacking and defending movements should not be rigid. Instead, they should be very adaptable. In the taiji movement "step forward, deflect down, intercept, and punch," students usually execute the movement correctly until the punch. The punch becomes a one-dimensional strike, rather than a more balanced technique that simultaneously attacks the torso and deflects with the opponent's punching arm.

Balance is not only important in kung-fu, it is also a valued concept of Chinese philosophy. Balance, in this sense, is synonymous with harmony. Likewise, the kung-fu practitioner who realizes balance in the broad Chinese sense may achieve harmony of body and mind.

To understand the Chinese meaning behind familiar terms, try to see past your assumptions and fixed ideas. The differences between the Chinese and Western cultures are significant, and these differences can manifest themselves in even our most basic thinking.

Take a step forward into your art. Use the Chinese definition of balance to measure all of your movements. Do it honestly, sincerely, and set a high standard. Don't be limited by fixed thinking. Though perfect harmony is seldom attained, do your best at least to find your balance. Then you won't be like a ballerina attempting gymnastics, or a football player charging around a basketball court. In other words, you will have learned to speak Chinese without an English accent.

Internal Training: Is It Necessary?

The internal arts related to kung-fu have become an obsession among many practitioners. They want to cultivate the inner energy that will make them invincible to their enemies, disease, and natural disasters. Many people refer to this internal training as qigong, meaning breathing exercise. but I prefer to call it neigong. *Nei* means internal, whereas *qi* refers to an aspect of neigong.

Neigong training is very important in martial arts. Chinese martial arts is based on two foundations: internal and external. If you take one and ignore the other, it's simply incomplete. If one or the other is carried to extremes, it can be harmful to the practitioner.

Neigong has broader application than just martial art. It can be divided into several different categories. "Immortal" neigong training supposedly transforms ordinary people into immortals. Healing neigong teaches people exercises that are investments for good health and life. Individuals in poor health can accelerate their recovery, and the neigong can be used in conjunction with Eastern and Western medicine. "Entertainment" neigong applies tricks and fakery to amuse people.

This trademark Hebei xingyi posture looks simple, but includes internal training.

Can anyone be antagonistic toward a magician who pulls out a dove or a rabbit from an empty hat? Everyone knows it's not real, but we all like to watch it.

None of these have much to do with martial arts neigong, however. Problems arise when people mix up the categories, sometimes trying to cheat and take advantage of others. They may attract more students and make more money but in the long run they are helping to destroy the real kung-fu.

Generally speaking, martial arts neigong falls into two different methods. Traditional Chinese martial arts possesses several hundred different fighting styles, which roughly can be divided into northern and southern. The two regions have unique ways to conduct and integrate internal practice into the styles.

Southern styles practice internal and external training from the very beginning. The movements are accompanied by audible breathing, vocalizations, and sounds connected with specific movements. In contrast, northern stylists concentrate on primarily the physical movement at the beginning. Neigong is introduced at later stages of development because it adds too much complexity at the onset of training. After all, beginners can't even manage their arms and legs yet.

Sometimes introducing neigong training too early causes trouble. If you do the neigong incorrectly, internal injury will sometimes result. Some teachers insist that their kung-fu students routinely take herbal medicine to counteract the effects of such training. My belief is that if you practice neigong correctly and gradually, this medical intervention won't be necessary. It's not totally wrong to begin by practicing internal and external training together, but students need good guidance and must practice very carefully.

Internal training begins with a fundamental principle: calm down, stay calm, and don't look outside but inward.

Internal training begins with a fundamental principle: calm down, stay calm, and don't look outside but inward. In xingyi-quan, for example, there's a famous posture called *san ti shi.* This

First level baji neigong: tapping the dantian with the fists.

trademark posture looks simple but also includes qigong training, breathing in and out in a controlled manner, somewhat like meditating.

Some people practice the *san ti shi* without ever practicing xingyi itself. The posture is relaxed and open. This practice has health benefits, but should not be confused with martial arts training. In martial arts, you can't afford to present an open door for your opponent. In addition to the breath exercise, the martial artist must sink the power to the *dantian* and also push it out the arms, in both outward and downward directions. The martial arts posture is squeezed, more compact, contracted, stretched, and twisted. If after ten years of "relaxed" postures you complain that you still can't generate power, in actuality you've never really tried.

Without movement, power must be generated from different directions combined. The legs and feet must be rooted, sending the energy down the legs, through the bottoms of the feet, deep into the earth. This internal training is common to all kung-fu styles, combining qigong breath exercises with sinking the power and radiating it in lateral directions.

The purpose of neigong is to get the entire body, not only the arms, involved in the movement. When my students practice basic neigong stance training, the coaches test them by pushing on their extended, rounded arms. If their arms bend and then push back, the movement is incorrect. Instead, the entire body as one unit must push from the back, waist, leg, feet, and the ground. Moreover, the body should react similarly if pushed anywhere, not just the arms.

In martial arts, the internal and external elements must be combined and developed through step-by-step training. Bajiquan, a famous northern style that was taught to bodyguards, includes extensive neigong training. At the first level, students breathe in the air and send it deep down into the dantian. The student then taps the dantian with finger tips or fists—sort of like a wake up call—and then push the air back out.

Now that the *dantian* has been discovered and awakened in level one, the fists are used to hit the *dantian* in the second level of training. Upon impact, the mind and *qi* are directed to the *dantian*. It could be said that the first level puts money *(qi)* into the *dantian* bank, and the second level checks to see how much has been accumulated.

The practitioner uses all the accumulated internal power to take a hit. In the beginning, the practitioner must seal the mouth and nose in order to draw all the *qi* into the *dantian*. At a high level, the practitioner can talk or sing, and it won't disturb the *qi* in the *dantian*.

At the third level, when the fists hit the *dantian,* the accumulated *qi* is sent out to other parts of the body. The special baji concussive stamping the ground with the legs adds vibration and helps deliver the *qi.* The practitioner develops the ability to send *qi* to any body part being threatened. The internal forces join the external to repel the attack, with *dantian* serving as the central station that dispenses the energy.

In contrast to the traditional martial arts of China, the modern wushu sanctioned by the mainland Chinese government lacks a balance of internal and external. For

Third level baji neigong: hitting the dantian *while stomping on the ground.*

pure entertainment I enjoy watching the athletes perform, but not a single move follows the correct kung-fu principles. The reasons for that empty kung-fu is because the modern wushu practitioners only have external training. If wushu replaces traditional training, the art of kung-fu will disappear over the next few generations.

In keeping with an era in which kung-fu is treated like an ancient treasure, many martial arts have been transformed into health exercises. This change is beneficial to all of society.

At this point, there hasn't been enough observation and accumulation of knowledge to allow for a solid comparison between real martial arts and the healing neigong practices. The healing neigong is more specialized in treating certain types of illness, developing specific kinds of energy, and strengthening the organs.

From my personal experience, I have found that you get more from traditional martial arts training. Martial arts neigong training addresses the entire body—all of the limbs and joints and internal organs. When your posture is tighter and your body squeezed and twisted, then your internal organs get massaged and exercised. Martial arts neigong can even be adapted to help special groups such as the elderly or those with serious health problems.

Much of our neigong training begins with qigong. I tell my students the breath is a bridge. After all, the internal organs don't really listen to your commands. You can tell your heart to stop but (hopefully) it won't. Likewise, you can order it to keep going but if it has made a decision to quit, your order will not be effective. The only organs with which you have some power of negotiation or control are your lungs. You can regulate the rate of breathing or hold your breath for a time. Although internal training isn't limited to the lungs, the breath bridges the external and internal worlds. It's a good place to start. After you cross the bridge to the internal territories, then you're in a good position to reap the rewards that come from further exploration and development.

Kung-fu Mind, Multi-dimensional Mind

Kung-fu techniques were created and refined over many centuries for the humble purpose of surviving life or death combat. During its long history a great deal of blood was shed by many masters, bodyguards, and soldiers who took part in the evolution of its sophisticated techniques. At the same time, a philosophy evolved to guide, enlighten, and enlarge our awareness and compassion. This was not the result of clever thinking, theory, and discussion. Instead, it sprang from action, experience, and feelings—the heart and soul of a people and their culture.

Most obviously, kung-fu offers a rigorous physical training that brings about many improvements in fitness, athletic ability, and self—defense for the hardworking student. To reach a high level, however, physical development must be accompanied by mental development. Without this element, even great strength, balance, speed, and endurance combined with excellent natural fighting instincts will not unlock the high levels of Chinese martial arts.

When a combat situation cannot be avoided, both the physical and mental aspects of kung-fu must be united in action.

Many people might mistakenly confuse mental and moral development. No one today can deny that our society from the top down needs a much stronger sense of ethics. The Chinese character *"wu"* (martial) is a combination of two other characters meaning "to stop the fight." In a nutshell, *"wu"* states kung-fu's fundamental moral instruction to all students: do not initiate combat, hurt others, or invade nations, but instead stop the fight and keep the peace. These high standards express the true value of martial arts.

In addition to physical and moral fitness, martial arts training helps people become socially and psychologically fit and fills huge gaps in our educational system. Many children can face a promising future thanks to changes in attitude and work habits learned from the martial arts. The moral, social, and psychological aspects of martial arts training are probably the biggest reason so many parents willingly sacrifice valuable free time to take their kids to classes several times a week.

Kung-fu practitioners operate from the center of the globe, interacting with their surroundings at all times.

When a combat situation cannot be avoided, both the physical and mental aspects of kung-fu must be united in action. The mind must be very agile, signaling the body to switch to alternate techniques in an instant. It must be flexible, stretching forward in time to anticipate an opponent's next moves. The mind must have endurance and stability, rescuing the fight at the very last minute under extreme duress. It must perceive and respond by pure reaction to several different inputs simultaneously.

The mind and body must coordinate much more than just arms and legs. Foot and knee, fist and elbow work in conjunction with hip and shoulder, and they are joined by the torso. In our fighting the body is not treated only as a potential target, to be guarded against any approach. Instead, the entire torso area, including the sides, back, and chest, is used to impact the opponent in a direct attack.

To understand this concept of whole-body fighting and the role of the mind, let's examine basic training. Leg training includes many kicking exercises. Students who wave their arms to balance during kicks are practicing at the lowest, most elementary level. The exercise performed with hands at the waist is an improvement but incomplete because aside from balance, it still doesn't contain much training beyond the kick itself. For a more complete practice, drop the arm of the kicking leg in front of the *dantian* and point the other arm to the rear in line with the shoulder, fist about ear height. It's not a complicated position, but it is difficult to maintain with any accuracy through a series of kicks. When a student delivers a good kick the instructor still might be critical because the back hand is in an incorrect position. This kind of requirement may seem strange, but the purpose is to extend the capacity of the mind to manage more than one point of awareness simultaneously.

Certainly many practitioners find these details annoying, irrelevant, and puzzling. After all, if your kick is correct and strong, what does it matter where you place your hands? Though martial arts promotional and instructional literature often talk about training the mind, many practitioners and instructors even choose to drop these details. In other words, they voluntarily sacrifice vital training that develops the mental abilities required for high-level kung-fu practice. As a result, the kung-fu fighting we see for the most part resembles other martial arts systems and contains few, if any, kung-fu techniques.

During a fight, students direct their attention forward towards the opponent. This is a natural human response that doesn't need to be taught. Most students fight under tournament rules that are safe, fair, controlled, and legal.

Kung-fu developed from situations where the fighter must pay attention to the entire space around them. Fairness is just a pretty idea to the individual who has to face several skilled opponents, possibly armed, attacking from different directions with the intention of murder. Those fighters were ruled by the laws of the jungle, not the laws of the tournament, and extraordinary skills were needed to survive.

Fighting the true kung-fu way requires expanded alertness, a multi-dimensional viewpoint that extends in all directions.

Many contemporary fighters feel their area of awareness covers a wide circle of space in front of them. In actuality, for most of them the boundary is much closer, just a little beyond their extended punching arm. From the kung-fu point of view, this is a one-dimensional, single-point plane of awareness. Fighting the true kung-fu way requires expanded alertness, a multi-dimensional viewpoint that extends in all directions.

Students need special training to push them beyond the limits imposed by their habits and assumptions.

The highest levels of kung-fu demand that we step beyond the arena of everyday consciousness and identities to adopt a 360-degree, global awareness that contains its own definitions for thought, action, response, and decision. Kung-fu practitioners operate from the center of the globe, interacting with their surroundings at all times. Through their knowledge of the global environment, they will also move it around to serve their needs.

This treasured relationship is one of interaction and respect, not dominance or submission. They bring heaven and earth together, moment to moment, forming the essential nobility potential to all human beings. For this, students need special training to push them beyond the limits imposed by their everyday habits and assumptions.

Global awareness can't be dissected in the laboratory or examined in detail through a slow-motion videotape. It is difficult to discuss because words alone can only provide hints that are easily misunderstood.

Global awareness is a state of mind and ability that can only be reached through hard work and an open attitude under the careful guidance of a qualified teacher. It is the space of multi-dimensional thought, reason, and experiential knowing, not our everyday mode of thinking about things and processing information. It is the space of living, not acting out an identity.

As children, we all possessed a sense of global awareness, but we lost this trait in the process of becoming "civilized" adults. Contemporary influences such as social structures, laws, peer pres-

A group of coaches from the author's Taiwan school practice siluchaquan.

sure, high-tech modern conveniences and the media have narrowed the mental abilities of many young people to one-dimensional thinking. Life unfolds step-by-step much like the linear progression of a computer program. Our society is producing generations of smart human robots. Traditional kung-fu can provide a way to keep open the child's door to other dimensions.

Children are our future. As adults, they will assume important positions as corporate executives, military commanders, political leaders, and parents. Leaders in both public and private sectors who can evaluate and act from a broader, deeper, more multi-dimensional viewpoint are desperately needed for the survival and good health of our world.

Otherwise, with incomplete training the desired results won't be achieved. Kung-fu is a bridge which allows every one of us the chance to merge the realm of philosophy with daily reality. Our rediscovered global awareness can create a bright future for our shared global village.

The Risk of Special Training

One crucial aspect of kung-fu training is for the practitioner to simultaneously develop in two main areas: technique and body conditioning. A practitioner perfects technique to be able to successfully avoid and defend against any manner of attack. Accordingly, with proper body conditioning, the practitioner is capable of administering and withstanding attacks without serious injury.

But what would it be like if the martial artist developed in one of these areas but not in the other? You may manage to strike an opponent and inflict damage, but unless your attacking hands are thoroughly conditioned, you'll suffer injuries that may make it impossible to continue fighting effectively. To make another comparison, no matter how well placed the attack, if you lack enough power, the effect on the opponent will be negligible. Similarly, great conditioning and power will allow you to inflict terrible damage, but such a skill matters little if the necessary knowledge of how to deliver the technique is lacking.

The ideal situation for the martial artist is to couple superior technique skills with proper and thorough conditioning.

Therefore, the ideal situation for the martial artist is to couple superior technique skills with proper and thorough conditioning. By working toward this goal, the practitioner can be confident that the technique will connect with the appropriate amount of power.

Kung-fu is not the only martial art that requires body conditioning as a supplement to refinement of technique. Just as many boxers train extensively on heavy bags and *karateka* on *maki-*

wara (striking post) to toughen their hands, some kung-fu styles emphasize practices such as iron-palm training to achieve similar results.

In ancient times the Chinese people systematically developed and perfected many unique ways to condition the body in order to withstand most kinds of attacks. The names used to refer to such practices were often exotic and unusual, such as "gold-bell coverage" and "iron-fabric shirt." Some of these intense conditioning programs were extremely difficult for the practitioner. Often the practitioners' bodies were irreversibly damaged, and they never reached the desired goal. These injuries usually didn't appear in the students' younger and stronger years, but emerged later on in life when their bodies naturally began to weaken. Although this kind of sacrifice and dedication was sometimes necessary in earlier times, present day students of kung-fu should not be encouraged to follow a path that may be destructive.

In this vein, the majority of extraordinary kung-fu skills that people have become accustomed to in movies are nothing more than fairy tales. We must acknowledge that the human body does have its physical limitations. Feats like jumping over rooftops, walking on water, and punching and kicking through solid stone are not products of our training but rather of our imaginations.

> *The majority of extraordinary kung-fu skills that people have become accustomed to in movies are nothing more than fairy tales.*

Qigong (breathing exercise) demonstrations, such as shattering massive stones or stopping one's heart from beating have gained popularity around the world. Even though these performers do practice long and hard hours to perfect their "supernatural" feats, they are in most cases only well-rehearsed tricks and good entertainment.

Some special conditioning exercises, such as iron palm, are legitimate and can still be learned today. It is of utmost importance that these be practiced carefully and patiently under the expert guidance of a qualified instructor. Generally speaking, the slower the training the more natural it is for the body.

Shortcuts or over-training can potentially lead to permanent injuries. Students who dedicate themselves to specialized body conditioning should always keep in mind the importance of the normal use of the hands. You shouldn't take your body for granted and risk permanent injury with improper attitude and practice. I have seen kung-fu practitioners who are unable to correctly hold chopsticks or a writing brush, all due to training incorrectly.

As a supplement to this type of special training, iron palm medicines can be helpful to a point; they encourage circulation and the healing of tissue that has been slightly damaged. Yet, if the injury is serious enough, the student must immediately consult a specialist for proper care and treatment.

Sifu Liu Yun Chiao teaching piquazhang bag strike exercises in the training hall for the bodyguards of President Chiang Kai-Shek.

Using iron palm medicines cannot be seen as a substitute for the specialized training exercises. There are no "iron-palm in 30 days" miracle medicines. And no matter how much an instructor charges for or raves about the superiority of a particular brand's exceptional properties, no medicine can guarantee 100-percent protection.

In summary, special training achieves no substantial results when it is not practiced in conjunction with technique. Yet equally, students should not get carried away with their training. The ultimate goal is not to be able to attempt or perform spectacular feats. Instead, special training serves as a supplement to enhance the martial artist's ability to develop technical skills.

Adapting Western Methods to Kung-fu

In any martial art or sport, a great deal of emphasis is placed on technique, the movements unique to a particular discipline. Reaching a high level of skill depends, in part, on the training methods that help one learn to do the techniques with skill and precision.

Sometimes students and teacher try to apply skills from one sport or martial art to another. In a general sense, having athletic ability is extensible, but each sport or martial art is distinguished by special techniques. The technique of throwing a baseball, for example, may have similarities to serving a tennis ball, but there are many obvious and subtle differences that make transferring techniques from baseball to tennis or vice versa a difficult process. Similarly, a well-trained karate practitioner may learn a kung-fu style, but he will inevitably perform the kung-fu techniques impurely (with a karate flavor) because his karate technique and training are so ingrained.

Baquazhang practitioners can practice the traditional circle walking techniques with weights attached to the arms.

In kung-fu, the techniques and training methods vary greatly even among the different styles. Each system has special techniques and its own flavor that set it apart from other styles. One should try to major in one style and fully develop the techniques within that system. Learning multiple kung-fu styles can become an obstacle to reaching a high skill level.

Practitioners should also be wary of adapting the basic training methods of one sport or martial art to another. Certainly all sports and martial arts have basic training methods to help students condition their bodies and gradually develop their technical skills. That training may include methods for improving flexibility, coordination, mobility, strength, stamina, and the ability to summon sudden, explosive bursts of power.

Some sports or martial arts, like karate and taekwondo, share similar training methods. But most sports and martial arts, because of the vast difference in the techniques and way the body is used, have specifically designed training methods that would not be helpful for learning other disciplines.

A problem arises when instructors devise their own training methods that mix the techniques and training methods of several martial arts. It's not uncommon to see a practitioner who does kung-fu forms, employs karate techniques for fighting, and trains in Western boxing. The result is a practitioner who can only become good in street fighting. The high-level fighting ability to be gained from concentrating fully on kung-fu is out of reach.

For the most part, Western training methods go against basic kung-fu principles and inhibit the students' progress.

For the most part, Western training methods go against basic kung-fu principles and inhibit one's students' progress. The difference in understanding and technique between East and West is clearly shown by the different ways the Chinese and Westerners utilize training methods such as bag punching and kicking, jogging, and rope jumping.

Jogging, for example, has become a popular form of exercise throughout the world. Some kung-fu practitioners jog to develop stronger legs and better stamina. Jogging in the usual way, however, does not help develop kung-fu.

In kung-fu, the body is ideally structured like a pyramid. This is the opposite of the Western ideal, where the body is narrow at the bottom and wide at the top. Western sports and exercise reinforce that top-heavy structure. One must have a strong foundation to do the techniques, so kung-fu has its own jogging methods to help develop this quality. In changquan (long fist), a special step called *xing bu* (movement step) is used for jogging. This step uses the legs to build stamina and forces the student to concentrate on developing the lower part of the body.

> *Kung-fu may be a traditional art, but that doesn't mean instructors should ignore some of the advances in training equipment.*

The development of jumping ability is important in kung-fu. It gives one training in changing the steps, rhythm, angle, and distance, and increases power and agility in the legs. Some practitioners skip rope to help their training. The method for jumping rope must follow the kung-fu principle of helping to sink the *qi* to the lower abdomen, and possibly combine usage training during practice. The tanglangquan (praying mantis style), for example, uses *san si bu* (triangle step) for conditioning. The practitioner's body stays at one low level with the arms in front protecting the frontal area. Only the legs change position as the practitioner jumps and lands in a different posture in the same stance.

Another example that shows the problem of adapting Western training methods to kung-fu involves the use of weights. By correctly practicing with weights, students can increase their strength and power, not only for a particular group of muscles, but for the whole body. Again, the idea is to develop the body in a kung-fu way, rather than build up massive muscles or try to set records for weightlifting.

Many practitioners employ iron rings along the wrist and forearm to help strengthen the limbs. The point isn't how much weight the student can handle, but how many times and how correctly he can do the technique without stopping. Using light weights and performing many repetitions lets the student practice techniques, build stamina, and develop strength. Baquazhang practitioners, for example, can practice the traditional circle walking techniques with weights attached to the arms.

The same principles hold true for using weights to improve weapons usage. Handling the sword requires a flexible, strong wrist. A simple way to develop and condition the wrist is to hold a piece of stone or brick in the fingers and move the object back and forth in a thrusting motion. In typical kung-fu fashion, the practice method incorporates technique and weight training.

Kung-fu may be a traditional art, but that doesn't mean instructors should be blind to some of the advances in training equipment. Instructors should take advantage of the modern training apparatus available today, such as Western weight training equipment. There is no reason to employ a horse-driven carriage in the age of the automobile just because it's more traditional.

Post training is an important part of the baguazhang system. The author "planted" nine posts in his Cupertino backyard, where they "grew" into a bagua forest.

In ancient China, weights usually consisted of a wooden stick with stones of equal weight placed at each end. Another Chinese weight-training device, called a stone log, has a wooden handle with a stone attached to it. The object is held in the hand as the practitioner does specific techniques.

Using ancient equipment is acceptable, but modern gear is safer and more convenient. One advantage of modern equipment is you can easily add or subtract weight without constructing a new apparatus. Some of the specially designed weight-training machines are particularly useful for improving techniques, as well as for helping one strengthen weak or injured areas.

There is an old Chinese saying: "You buy the beautiful wooden box, and return the pearl." This expression points out the danger of incorrectly adapting Western training methods or techniques to kung-fu. If you practice kung-fu incorrectly, all you have is a fancy box that says "Made in China." To obtain the pearl, you must understand the goal of the training and follow the real kung-fu principles in your daily practice.

Part 6

Usage: The Soul of Kung-fu

The Kung-fu Art of Fighting

Fighting is a natural, instinctive human trait. You don't need to learn a formal martial art to survive (or perish) in the street. You can acquire some basic fighting skills by simply getting together and practicing with people informally, without the aid of a certified instructor. In fact, many who claim to be martial artists are merely experienced street fighters, relying mostly on natural ability rather than technique to overpower an opponent.

Of course, the purpose of a martial art is to win the fight by whatever means necessary. However, it's a fact that the "natural," unschooled type of fighter is invariably defeated by a superior technician. And as in any other "art," the raw materials (in this case, the human body and mind) are refined and developed to a high level, as shown in the skill and expertise of the artist's work.

Genuine martial art is quite different from "natural" fighting, just as poetry is different from more natural, conversational forms of writing. In both cases you need a certain attitude and special training to learn such an art.

In 1992, weapons free-sparring was introduced to tournaments throughout the U.S. by the Traditional Wushu Association, a non-profit organization founded by the author.

Kung-fu, therefore, is not a "natural" way to fight per se. It becomes natural only after extensive training that washes away the remnants of so-called natural fighting habits, as well as those acquired from other activities such as sports or dance.

Kung-fu is an art of fighting, not just a fighting art. The distinction implied here is that kung-fu emphasizes a special way of using the body to deliver not only power, but also complex, sophisticated, multiple-attacking techniques, as well as combat strategies that utilize the knowledge gained from centuries of battlefield experience.

Genuine martial art is quite different from "natural" fighting, just as poetry is different from natural, conversational forms of writing.

Learning the kung-fu way to fight is a difficult and lengthy process. It's not a discipline that can be absorbed exclusively from books, magazines, movies, or by trial-and-error—you need a qualified instructor.

Most students of kung-fu (or any other martial art) devote significant time and effort to perfect their techniques and forms, concentrating on learning to move in ways defined by their particular style. Some can do forms very well and even show an understanding of the application (or usage). However, when involved in sparring, many often revert to natural fighting.

Each year, numerous contestants in different tournaments and divisions are awarded cups, plaques, medals, or certificates for kung-fu sparring. If we examine tournament sparring more closely, however, we see almost exclusively natural fighting or techniques from other martial arts systems, such as boxing, karate, taekwondo, and judo.

Several ideas might explain why most students are unable to apply their techniques in spontaneous sparring or fighting situations. The fundamental reason is that students (and some instructors) do not probe deep enough beneath the surface of their art, and instead are easily satisfied and complacent.

Some students who want to learn fast immediately begin sparring. They treat kung-fu like a fast-food item to buy and consume as quickly as possible. They cannot stand to wait, whether it's for an opportunity to attack or for an understanding of the training process. This attitude only limits the potential of students. One must give up any previous conceptions about fighting and instead follow the established kung-fu way to train. Simply stated, kung-fu is a lifestyle and a life study.

Kung-fu is the art of fighting, not just a fighting art.

The method for achieving this goal is to follow the step-by-step training that has been developed over the centuries by martial artists. By applying oneself to the basics, the new habits become "natural." This process may take one or several years to reach, depending on the individual student.

In general, basics and all other mid-level training methods are a preparation for sparring training. *Sanshou* (individual movement training) is traditionally used as a preface to sparring. At first, students pair off and practice individual techniques or combinations. In the beginning, tactics are predetermined so that both participants know the approximate striking areas and sequences. At the more advanced level of *sanshou,* the striking areas and sequences are less predetermined, thus preparing the student for free sparring.

The purpose of this training is not to "win the fight." Since students must cooperate with one another by providing feedback to

The author demonstrates Chinese sword fighting techniques during the Master's Demonstration and Exchange at the 1991 Jinan (China) Traditional Wushu Festival.

make sure the techniques are done correctly. The instructor can also work with students at this stage, helping to fine-tune technique and improve understanding of the usage.

Sparring training must be carefully monitored by the instructor, and students should use safety equipment. Pure kung-fu sparring, unlike other martial arts, doesn't yet have any established safety rules governing free fighting.

Unfortunately, these traditional concepts and training principles are followed by only a few instructors in the last several decades. Indeed, few practitioners of the last three generations actually knew how to use their kung-fu in real-life situations. Thus, today it is unusual to find instructors who can fully understand and apply their kung-fu.

Some instructors have let their art die out while others teach forms or fighting without passing on the real usage. At the same time, some instructors who don't know how to fight the kung-fu way often teach "street fighting" or use other martial arts such as karate, which have more easily usable techniques and systematic training methods. All the while, such people continue to call their art kung-fu, adding to the already substantial mass of misconceptions.

This trend is further complicated by other factors. Even if the instructor knows the real usage, there is no standardized program for teaching this while at the same time giving the proper sparring training. Every style and instructor has different methods for achieving that goal. Also, sparring training is often less interesting than forms instruction (hence the emphasis on fancy forms today, rather than basics and usage). The reasons?

Some instructors simply want to survive economically (or don't know real usage) so they satisfy the students' appetite by serving them whatever they like. Instructors amuse their students by giving them sparring too early, before the correct habits have formed. Equally, students can be seduced into thinking that knowing many forms enables them to fight.

Often prearranged, two-person forms and push-hands training are overemphasized. Prearranged forms merely simulate actual fighting situations but they are not a substitute for sparring because you practice or perform with a partner, not an enemy. In fact, spending too much time on this type of training severely compromises your ability to fight.

Usage is the soul of kung-fu, and sparring training is an essential element to acquire skill in and an understanding of usage. But one must go through the step-by-step training to reach that high goal as there are no shortcuts. With a full immersion in kung-fu study and with a serious attitude, the pure flavor of the art can come out—once you move, you move naturally in the manner of whatever kung-fu style learned.

Real Kung-fu: Use It or Lose It!

Although kung-fu today is a great multi-purpose art, everyone who practices kung-fu should know its real usage. Practitioners can know the basic usage, but making the techniques instinctive, automatic reflexes are necessary and one of the most challenging aspects of kung-fu.

> *In kung-fu fighting, many techniques require use of the entire arm, not only the fist or palm.*

All martial arts styles have their own specialized techniques, and training methods for developing the correct fighting habits. Teachers preparing their pupils to fight in the ring must design different ways to develop students' potential, strengthen their basics, and polish their blocking, attacking, ducking, and approaching abilities. Boxers, for instance, jump rope to prepare themselves to bounce in any direction during a match. In taekwondo *dojang* (training halls), practitioners train hard to kick higher than their heads because that's the way to score in tournaments. In other words, they practice techniques that they need to use in fighting.

Kung-fu practitioners train very hard too but much of the time it's wasted. For example, kung-fu students and teachers have a universal faith in the ability of the horse stance to develop kung-fu. The horse stance does build up leg muscles and stability, but this foundation training is indispensable only if we learn to fight the kung-fu way. Kung-fu fighting is not point fighting, allowing only fists and heels to punch or kick a target. In kung-fu fighting, many techniques require use of the entire arm, not only the fist or palm; similarly, many techniques require use of the entire leg, not only the kicking foot. Kung-fu also requires that the elbow and knee coordinate with the hand and foot as instruments of usage. Furthermore, any part of the body can be used as a means of attack and impact.

How can practitioners judge if their own sparring styles contain real kung-fu usage? Likewise, how can spectators tell whether competitors are fighting the kung-fu way?

Looking for authentic kung-fu usage can be difficult. Kung-fu simply has too many styles and different ways to fight. Secondly, no one in history ever learned all the different styles and then drew any conclusions that would lead to codifying kung-fu techniques. Nonetheless, I will try to offer a few principles that differentiate kung-fu from other methods of fighting.

Real kung-fu is close-in fighting, and internal body twisting is used to generate the power.

When you see a kung-fu fighter issuing blocking or attacking movements with definite, strong purpose, you might enjoy the clarity of the technique, but that's not kung-fu.

In kung-fu, the initial movement usually does not show clear purpose. It is designed to draw the opponent's reaction. From that point, the practitioner responds with the appropriate single movement or combination, and judges from the opponent's reaction whether to switch to another technique. Good kung-fu technique is not black and white—it won't show definite blocks or strikes, and usually doesn't even have a clear, predetermined target. The kung-fu practitioner must always be ready to change techniques. Although a movement might look simple, it contains many potential alternatives, and can be used both to attack and defend at the same time.

When you see a kung-fu fighter launch a hand strike and then, whether hit or miss, voluntarily pull the hand backward to deliver a second attack, that's not kung-fu.

In kung-fu, once the arm is launched forward to attack or defend, it shouldn't voluntarily be withdrawn. No matter the outcome of the movement, the arm should change to another technique without interruption. For example, if the hand succeeds in striking the target, an elbow strike and a shoulder blow follow. Or after the initial hand strike, without bending the arm the fighter will twist the waist to deliver the second hit, then twist the heel (without withdrawing the hand) and deliver the third hit. If the attack isn't successful, the hand then immediately transfers to other techniques without pulling back for a new start.

When you see a kung-fu fighter treat a blocked attack as finished, continuing on to other techniques without realizing there are still many possibilities left within the initial attack, that's not kung-fu.

In kung-fu, one hand almost never acts alone. Practitioners must work hard to build up a natural reaction in which the hand, elbow, and shoulder always provide continuous mutual support. If a punch is blocked by the opponent's forearm, then it should stick with the forearm and, using it as a support, turn the elbow to change the direction or angle of the arm and twist the shoulder to deliver another strike with the same hand.

Only circular motions can redirect the opponents momentum and get the door open.

When you see a kung-fu fighter using hand or leg to carry out and complete the techniques while at the same time never engaging the entire body as an essential contributor to any part of the usage, that's not kung-fu.

149

In kung-fu, single-targeted movements are rare. Usually two or three movements in different areas will be launched simultaneously. For example, the hand gets the opponent's door open, allow-

ing the hip to deliver a powerful impact; based on the opponent's reaction to this onslaught, the elbow strikes and the leg sweeps like a scissors to smash him to the ground. In this technique, each section of the body cooperates with all the others to administer a complete attack. In other words, this single usage is executed by all different parts of our body.

In kung-fu, high kicks are for training and low kicks for real usage.

When you see a kung-fu fighter aim most kicks above the waist, that's not kung-fu.

In kung-fu we kick high for training and low for real usage. The emphasis is on invisible kicking. First of all, it's difficult to spot a low kick coming in. Secondly, arm engagements are used to distract the enemy and conceal lower body activities so that a powerful kick can be delivered from underneath.

When you see kung-fu fighters always using kicks to lead the fight, that's not kung-fu.

In kung-fu, the fighting engagement does not normally begin with a kick. Instead, the forceful, leading kick is almost always delivered after the opponent's door has been opened, or after retreating from several punches or after falling. These situations create a comfortable distance which allows a powerful kick to conclude the fight.

When you see a kung-fu fighter throwing many kicks but neglecting the step during the fight, that's not kung-fu.

In kung-fu, kicking is only one portion of leg technique. Much more important and powerful than the kick is the step. The step places the fighter in the correct position, moving forward, backward, sideways, and twisting. It also moves the leg starting from the foot on up the ankle, shin, knee, thigh, and hip to employ multiple usage, such as guarding, trapping, hitting, lifting, sweeping, and scooping.

When you see a kung-fu fighter rely only on thrusting arms and an enlarged distance to produce a powerful punch and voluntarily abandon the body's ability to cooperate with the arm for power-issuing, that's not kung-fu.

In kung-fu, power issuing doesn't rely on an externally enlarged working distance and space. Real kung-fu is close-in fighting, and internal body twisting is used to generate the power. For example, even though an arm has already been straightened, there's no need to bend it so that the fist can withdraw in preparation for a strong punch. The kung-fu way is to twist the heel, knee, waist, shoulder, elbow, and wrist as one well-formed unit. Strong power can thus be generated from the ground up to hit the target.

When you see a kung-fu fighter execute techniques primarily in a straight line, rarely if ever using a curved movement, then that's not kung-fu.

In kung-fu most movements are circular, curved, or twisting. Though you sometimes see a straight hand strike, the waist is usually turning and the legs are twisting. For the clearest example, pay attention to arm movements. Only circular motions can redirect the opponent's momentum and get the door open. This creates an approach right into the opponent's space where close-in fighting takes place. Then the elbows, knees, shoulder, and hip can join in the fight. At the same time, this kind of twisting and circling movement brings the usage and power issuing together as one.

The kung-fu way to fight truly embodies the meaning of "kung-fu." Hard work and patience over a long period of time are required to internalize the principles I have outlined. Those practitioners and instructors who are dedicated and honest enough to face the sweat, pain, and frustrations necessary to learn the kung-fu way of fighting will be greatly rewarded.

Use Your Head, Not Your Opponent's

When people fight, they usually start by attacking their opponent's face. You see this trait everywhere: kids fighting in a schoolyard, teenagers brawling in the street, adults exchanging blows in a bar. As common as face attacks are, however, they shouldn't be the trained martial artist's only fighting technique. Yet, even highly qualified martial artists insist on repeatedly attacking their opponent's face.

Generally, a martial artist's punching and kicking power exceeds that of the untrained fighter. Surprisingly, the martial artist's concept of how to fight is often indistinguishable from the lay person's fighting notion. This fact is disheartening and difficult to understand.

If you try to attack your opponent's lower body after attacking his head, your middle area will be open to your opponent's attack.

I understand that fights usually begin with foul words, so it's easy to understand that when people fight, they want to destroy each other's transmitter of hostile messages. Furthermore, most people know the face or head can be severely damaged in a fight. An angered fighter often strikes the face hoping for a knockout, or at least a damaging blow to the eyes, nose or other vulnerable head areas. Even for an accomplished martial artists, the face and head are ultimate targets. When you can attack your opponent's head, take the opportunity.

The face, however, isn't always open to a punch or kick. In fact, because the face is usually well protected, you must open it up to your attack.

The question of where to strike touches on basic differences between Asian and Western cultures. The upper body has always been important to Western martial artists, who attack the head or torso and, for whatever reason, don't like attacking below the belt. Likewise, Western martial artists guard the upper body and leave the lower body unprotected. Western martial artists rely on arm and hand techniques more than leg techniques. Of course, you can argue that Western martial artists use their legs for support and that their leg movement is coordinated with their hand movement. But if you compare this limited concept of leg movement with the legs' role among Asian martial artists, you can see why boxing didn't originate in the East.

Asian martial arts, such as kung-fu, reflect the cultures that gave them birth. One facet of Eastern culture is treating the body as a whole, and Eastern martial artists generally follow this principle. They believe all areas of the body are equally important targets, and they're trained to use their own, and their opponent's, entire body during combat. Survival is the root of Eastern fighting. In line with Eastern tradition, there are no rules; it's do or die. Fighters attack the whole body, not just the face.

Let's examine a kung-fu principle. Kung-fu stylists divide the human body into three levels: low, middle, and high. These levels

are respectively referred to as Earth, man, and Heaven. Kung-fu fighters attack all three levels, as well as protect all three levels. A fighter's goal is to penetrate the holes in an opponent's defense while making sure their own defense is sound.

The middle area is considered the best place to start an attack. After a mid-dle-level attack, your oppo-

These students in China practice shoulder-level punches.

nent's head and lower body are open targets. The number of possible techniques is doubled.

If you first attack your opponent's head, the situation is different. Your only real option is to strike your opponent's middle area. Don't attack your opponent's lower body after you strike his head. The lower body is too far away from the head, and it takes too long to strike low and then strike high. If you try to attack your opponent's lower body after attacking his head, your middle area will be open to your opponent's attack. Similarly, if you first attack low, the only option for a second strike is to attack the middle area.

A middle-level attack takes full advantage of your body's power. An upward punch works against gravity, and therefore requires more energy than a level or downward punch. Beginning martial arts students usually find shoulder-level punching uncomfortable—even painful—because they want to punch at eye level. Students should make shoulder level punching second nature.

To summarize, the concept of Heaven, Earth, and man is central to Chinese and other Asian philosophies. Man is the most important level. If he follows Heaven's rule (Tao), the Earth benefits, and peace and happiness abound. The concept of Heaven, Earth, and man is applied in many areas of Asian culture, but in kung-fu, it manifests itself in low, middle, and high targets.

The Continuous Fist

All martial artists train to develop the use of the hand. Some systems, such as tanglangquan (praying mantis) and baihe (white crane) kung-fu are readily identifiable by their distinctive hand techniques. Instructors often emphasize using the hand in various formations such as palms, fists, and hooks. While these hand techniques are useful, more emphasis should be placed on using the entire arm. All good systems of kung-fu make use of the whole arm. Some kung-fu systems do not train for whole arm use, a tradeoff that allows for more rapid learning but less skill longer term.

Treating the whole arm as the fist enables one to attack and defend simultaneously.

The Chinese say "the whole arm is the fist." This holds true regardless of the position of the hand. The hand functions like a drill bit and the arm like the drill motor, coordinating with the entire body. The Chinese even consider "the whole body is the fist." Students must comprehend using the body as a single unit.

In kung-fu, all techniques are seen in terms of the whole body, never as a single point. This whole body approach to martial art is rooted in the psychological heritage of China. The lung (mistakenly translated into English as dragon) is symbolic of the Chinese character and good fortune. It is an entity composed of the most diverse creatures: horse, eagle, ox, snake, deer, fish. The Chinese mind revels in the unification of the whole, and kung-fu aims to unify the entire body.

Chan si jin (silk reeling energy) is required to use the entire body in the most efficient way. Whole body training begins with the use of the arm, which provides a large area for defensive maneuvers as well as attacking and controlling an opponent. The entire arm is in readiness, prepared for spontaneous adjustment. If one's hand is parried, it can be followed by the elbow and shoulder, like the connected cars of a train.

Treating the whole arm as the fist enables one to attack and defend simultaneously. In fact, use of the whole arm allows one to wait for an opponent to strike first and then "beat him to the punch." A common example of this is to use one's forearm and elbow to deflect an attack as the other hand simultaneously strikes.

The arm has three sections: the root, which is the shoulder area; the middle, which pertains to the elbow area; and the front, which is the hand in any position.

The hand functions like a drill bit and the arm like the drill motor, coordinating with the entire body.

Techniques for defense and attack make use of the three sections to create the *men* (door), which is the entrance to an opponent's vulnerable area. Once an opponent's door has been opened, the kung-fu practitioner enters with the intention of gaining not a mere temporary advantage but control of the opponent to terminate the conflict.

Weapons in kung-fu are used differently than in all other martial arts systems. They are considered an extension of the arm, and are also classified similarly in three sections: root, middle, and front. An understanding of the uses of the arm's three sections makes it possible to grasp genuine empty-hand and weapon usage.

Skill in use of the whole arm is not easily attainable. The ability to concentrate on and use several parts of the body at the same time comes only with dedication, patience, and adept instruction.

Considerable sparring training is essential for whole arm usage. While sparring students must not revert to old habits or use single-point techniques that are counter to the basic principles.

The Chinese say the kung-fu person "can see four directions and hear eight actions." This adage is not to be taken literally but does approximate the degree of sensitivity and awareness necessary for an accomplished kung-fu practitioner. We should all strive to fulfill this high goal, and make the whole body a fist.

The Nine Doors of Kung-fu

The foes measure each other. Though they are opponents, their goal is identical: to destroy one another. Dangerous possibilities fill their minds. "Shall I attack what seems to be an opening, or does a trap await? Shall I invite his attack, thereby setting my own trap?" In this game a mistake can be fatal, but to hesitate could also prove disastrous.

In the swift and spontaneous action of combat, no strategy or technique is guaranteed success. For every attack, there is an effective counterattack. In the scene described, both combatants seek a target, but likewise present themselves as targets. The dilemma is to reach the enemy without putting yourself in jeopardy: attack without relinquishing safety.

The arm is a fighter's first line of defense and the most adaptable and skilled part of the body.

By analyzing the relationship between combatants, the ancient Chinese created the concept of the door, called *men* in Chinese. They divided the body and the area around the body into three sets of doors.

One set constitutes the vertical plane and is divided into the upper, middle, and lower portions of the body. This is the most natural way of dividing the body, and is obvious even to those people without any kung-fu training. The horizontal plane is divided into the center of the body and the left and right sides. The last set of the three doors—outer, middle, and inner—manifests the dimension of the other doors relative to the body.

The concept of the nine doors is used to explain how one maintains a secure defense while penetrating, or creating a leak, in

Horizontal doors.

the enemy's defense. The designation of the high, middle, and low doors is subject to a certain amount of change. An alteration is achieved primarily when a low defensive position is taken. By assuming a low stance the vertical doors is reduced from three to two. This concept can be explained either as eliminating the upper door or the middle door. A low stance drops the entire body; and the upper door area is vacated. The other way of looking at the situation is to say that in a low stance the middle door is so well guarded that it is virtually absent, leaving only the upper and lower doors. The only other possibilities for altering the vertical door relationship between opponents is for one to crouch or jump.

The doors of the horizontal plane are more variable. Although the left and right side of one's body can't actually change, the relationship between the sides of two moving bodies alter frequency. Protecting the left and right doors and gaining access to the opponent is accomplished by finding the advantageous angle. This is similar to a situation where opposing tanks each try to maneuver the other into exposing its broad and weakly protected side.

In kung-fu, reaching the opponent is not an end in itself, but one of a series of steps that require patience and foresight.

The concept of protecting one's center is taught in all styles by most martial artists. The outer, middle, and inner doors seem to be emphasized only in kung-fu. The outer door is the space immediately beyond a fighter's extended arms; which an opponent attempts to bridge.

The time interval before contact occurs is considered by kung-fu practitioners as most dangerous. Until contact is effected, the opponent's intent is unclear. As long as uncertainty prevails this condition is ripe with danger. Once contact is achieved the kung-fu practitioner can feel the opponent and has a direct sense of their movement and intent.

The Chinese call the procedure for initiating contact, *chiao men,* which means to "knock on the door." The basic idea of knocking on the door is to make the enemy react, either by eliciting a response to a fake or authentic attack, or by inviting an attack by presenting an apparent opening. Either way, contact is achieved.

In kung-fu, reaching the opponent is not an end in itself, but one of a series of steps that require patience and foresight. The

well-trained kung-fu practitioner should be able to see in advance the next two, three, or four moves, and shouldn't be seduced by an opportunity to inflict only partial damage.

Kung-fu techniques do not produce a clash of force against force. Instead, the arm is used in a shaving-like action to deflect an attack or to maintain maximum contact while attacking. An example of the latter would be countering an attack by sliding one's arm along the opponent's attacking arm, using the forearm and elbow to deflect the attack as a fighter's fist strikes the opponent.

The arm is a fighter's first line of defense and the most adaptable and skilled part of the body. Therefore, numerous techniques have been devised for using the entire arm for both attacking and defending. The kung-fu practitioner wants to get as much of the arm as possible in contact with the opponent's in order to eventually gain control.

Vertical doors.

After contact is established, three significant skills are utilized to reach the enemy's middle and inner doors. These skills are *peng jing* (outward energy), *nian jing* (sticking energy), and *ting jing* (listening energy). They are integral to both kung-fu bare-hand and weapons usage.

Beng jing is a fundamental energy in kung-fu. It is outward energy or pressure, a kind of expansive property spread throughout the body that may be expressed in a movement. Though *peng jing* exists everywhere, it can't be triggered without contact. *Beng jing* is like a water color saturating, more or less evenly, a piece of paper. However, once a particular point on the paper is touched that point

becomes darker. In this way, *peng jing* is like a system of sensitive explosive charges; if the *peng jing* is strong enough to diminish the force of the attack, a counterattack can be mounted.

Nian jing is the ability to adhere to and follow an opponent's movement. This kind of "sticking" energy allows one to interfere with an opponent's movement by sensing the changes in positioning.

The practitioner using *nian jing* understands that combat is a dynamic, ever-changing conflict relationship.

Inner to outer doors.

Fighting with a human is not like attacking a sandbag. Fixed plans often bring unwanted results. *Nian jing* requires staying in contact with an opponent, allowing one to react spontaneously rather than insisting on premeditated plan.

Ting jing is tactile sensitivity. In the outer and middle door area, furious arm interplay takes place as opponents try for superior position. *Ting jing* is used to feel an opponent's movement and pressure. It requires "reading" the opponent's intention through one's sense of touch, as well as feeling the opportunity to get in their door.

When in contact with an opponent, one must remain calm and relaxed. The practitioner with a tense, rigid body is not capable of much *ting jing*. When one is relaxed and dynamically flexible, rigidity and obstinate force will almost surely lead to an opponent's defeat.

As opponents draw ever closer, the kung-fu practitioner's concern for losing contact with a foe becomes more pronounced. At such close quarters, a strike can reach its target almost instantaneously. Reading and following the opponent's movement, the practitioner is alert to the slightest opening, and ready to smother an attack almost before it begins. Even a low kick or knee strike can be sensed through arm contact by a practitioner with good *ting jing.*

From the proximity of the inner door, the entire body can be used for attacking. The practitioner must possess awareness of not only the arm but of the entire body, and be able to simultaneously divide his or her attention between different areas. In addition to the commonly used parts of the body such as the hand, elbow, knee, and foot, at close range the shoulder, hip, and lower leg come into play.

> *Reading and following the opponent's movement, the practitioner is alert to the slightest opening, and ready to smother and attack almost before it begins*

Although the shoulder and the hip probably won't be used to deliver the finishing blow, they are frequently used to slam against the opponent, opening the way for the killing technique. From a defensive standpoint, the upper arm and shoulder are used to deflect or defuse the force of a blow that has penetrated to a fighter's inner door.

The concept of the nine doors is the basis of mastering kung-fu as a martial art. Without this essential element, kung-fu is merely an empty shell, void of its soul.

Part 7

Masters and Students

How to Choose a Kung-fu Teacher

The field of kung-fu includes a vast spectrum of styles. Each one has a special flavor and unique characteristics, depending on the origin of the style and the particular emphasis of the teacher. Given the number of variables, choosing a style and an instructor can be a difficult process. Not only are kung-fu styles diverse, but each teacher is different, and so are the needs of each student. The key is to match your needs with the right style and teacher.

The task of searching for a teacher is like trying to find a rare treasure that will enhance your life mentally and physically.

Unlike other martial arts, kung-fu has evolved over the centuries without developing any organized network to standardize and promote the traditional arts. As a result, there is a lack of uniformity of styles and teaching methods. The task of searching for a teacher is like trying to find a rare treasure that will enhance your life mentally and physically. Time and patience are required to learn kung-fu, and these qualities are also necessary in seeking out a teacher.

The first step on the path to finding a teacher is to honestly assess your own abilities and needs. Identify the main reason for becoming involved in kung-fu, and then direct the search in that specific area. For this purpose it is useful to define the basic categories of kung-fu training.

As an art form, kung-fu emphasizes performing and the aesthetic qualities of the movements. A focus on exercise promotes the

Sifu Li Kun San, the highest generation mantis master in Taiwan, helped the author clear up his questions and finalize his practice in the praying mantis style.

health benefits and overall body conditioning. Finally, a martial focus stresses practical application and usage.

These categories provide a focus for inquiry, helping to define an area of kung-fu that will be most appropriate. For people with only limited exposure to kung-fu, it is worthwhile to investigate all the categories. This may involve visiting or participating in classes, going to demonstrations, talking with senior students and instructors, and reading whatever is available in books or magazines. If there is difficulty in locating the kung-fu teachers in your community, then check the phone directory, and the directories in martial arts publications. Keeping a written record during this initial period of searching may help in discovering what style and category of kung-fu is of most interest to you.

However, those who are new to kung-fu can easily be misled by relying solely on yellow pages, kung-fu movies, and kung-fu fairy tales found in magazine and books. If at all possible, find someone with enough experience to help you avoid being seduced by unqualified teachers with slick on-stage demonstrations and trophy collections.

You should learn as much as you can about China. Plan your next vacation to China. Becoming involved with your local Chinese community and organizations can open up many doors that could lead to a teacher. Take classes, read books, study Chinese literature and history, and go to movies (not kung-fu movies-they can only give you the wrong message) to expand your horizons.

You should also check out other martial arts related to kung-fu: ju-jutsu, judo, karate, aikido, and taekwondo. Although they originate in other Asian countries, they are much more modernized, systematized, and popularly accepted throughout the world than kung-fu. These arts can be a useful aid to gaining an understanding of Chinese martial arts because they have similar cultural roots, some elements of kung-fu, and, more importantly, are much easier to find. In addition, knowledge of the original spirit, theory, technique, and appearance of other Asian martial arts can help you a great deal to spot traditional kung-fu styles and their masters.

> *Take classes, read books, study Chinese literature and history, and go to movies (not kung-fu movies—they can only give you the wrong message) to expand your horizons.*

Upon deciding what category is most suitable, you can investigate further by revisiting classes and meeting with students and teachers. It is important to treat this process seriously, evaluating both your own skills and needs and the expertise and teaching skills of the various teachers.

My experience training in Taiwan illustrates the importance of this process. I wasted a great deal of time and money during my search for the right teacher. Sometimes I was cheated by unqualified instructors. It is not the amount of money spent, but the time that is precious. If you spend a long time with the wrong teacher, it is like squandering your abilities and getting only the fool's gold. This is a problem not only in Taiwan, but also in other Asian countries and the U.S. From this experience I have formulated some guidelines to help evaluate a teacher and school for each of the three categories.

Performing art

The easiest category to evaluate is for those primarily interested in kung-fu as a performing art. Since this area of concentration emphasizes the enjoyment and aesthetic value of the movements, the main guideline for choosing a style is personal taste. Upon finding an appealing style, join the class for a period of time to see if it is the appropriate style and instructor for you.

It is not only necessary to assess the teacher's ability to teach, but also to consider whether you can do the particular kind of movement that attracts you. The beautiful movements from a kung-fu form may look simple, but may take many years of practice to perfect. Many times what is appealing to the eyes may not suit the body type and temperament of the student. After a few months of practice a frank discussion with the teacher should help you assess the situation and decide if it's going to be possible to develop within that system.

Exercise

Some students may want to stress just the exercise aspect of kung-fu, concentrating on stretching, strengthening, conditioning, and health benefits in general. As a guideline, the prospective student should find out if the instructor has any background in health-related fields such as massage, acupuncture, Chinese herbal medicine, or physical education. While watching a class, observe how the other students perform. See if the instructor teaches anything that contradicts fundamental health principles. If you feel you are too inexperienced to judge, then try to find a more knowledgeable friend to assist in this process. Of course, you can always try out a class, and if it proves to be unsuitable look for another.

Many times the most qualified teachers are not professional kung-fu instructors nor are they trying to acquire a reputation.

Martial art

The most difficult category in choosing a teacher and style is the area of martial art. As I mentioned before, the lack of a centralized organization and common standards make it difficult to obtain dependable information. Many times the most qualified teachers are not professional kung-fu instructors nor are they trying to acquire a reputation. And, unfortunately, many unqualified instructors are teaching and promoting a great many misconceptions about kung-fu, especially in the area of self-defense.

Conversely, you may hear about teachers who insist they know nothing about kung-fu. You beg them face to face to teach you, but they will still refuse.

The problem for the inexperienced student is how to evaluate the skill and authenticity of the teacher. Following are some basic guidelines that can help in this process. As usual, attending classes and demonstrations, speaking with students and teachers, and contacting other available sources of information is important. Try to learn as much as possible about the teacher's background. Checking the teacher's lineage might give an indication of his rank, extent of training, and knowledge of kung-fu usage.

No matter if the instructor is reluctant to answer questions or answers these questions in great detail, there is no guarantee that the information is correct. Some instructors are very humble, and unassuming, while others boast of their supposed accomplishments. Sometimes it is possible to verify such information from other sources, such as books. This process of investigation may be tedious, but it is essential. It worked for me in Taiwan, and should be applied in this country where there is even more chance of being steered in the wrong direction.

It is most important to find both the right teacher and the right style. The teacher and style together can motivate the student to practice and improve. Even so, sometimes the style does not fit the body type and personality of the student. The student should be flexible in this respect, changing to another style or instructor if necessary.

In any aspect of kung-fu, teachers should make the development of students their first priority, and should not try to hold back information or deceive. Students should respect the experience and tradition of the teacher. In this way the two can grow together, and achieve their respective goals. Remember, once you embark on a serious search for the right teacher and style, your kung-fu training has already begun.

Only a Kung-fu Teacher

I really enjoy teaching kung-fu. I meet all kinds of people who are interested in learning from me. Curiously, I've found that some people arrive at my classes with motives other than learning kung-fu. Some are actually looking for a father figure, or someone to act as their big brother—they want someone to take care of them.

I also encounter people who have been powerfully influenced by kung-fu movies. They see me as a leader of some Chinese gang. They intend to dedicate their ability, money, energy, and whole being to the survival of our gang in the face of threatening enemy schools.

Some others treat me like a novel representative of Asian culture, charmed by my less-than-perfect English, different habits, and traditions.

And some want to continue their elementary school education, with me as their nice teacher. They are eager to hear my encouragement: "I'm so proud of you," "Oh, what a fine job," or "That's just wonderful." Flattery and compliments are the pillars of their contentment.

Finally, there are people who want to believe my past is marked by unmentionable deeds and that my mission here in the United States, concealed behind the veil of a kung-fu instructor, is secret. "How many have you killed?," they want to know. "Weren't you an assassin? What is your discreet relationship with a certain underground army? And tell me," they inquire, "what is your real purpose in the United States?"

I do like meeting new and different people, but I don't think I provide much enjoyment for the type of people mentioned. Invariably, I fall short of their expectations.

You see, I'm nothing but a kung-fu teacher. Actually, that's not my whole life. I have a family, the typical variety of relationships, and I like making friends. I'm no different than the person next door.

In fact, I am the guy next door, and I enjoy my neighborhood. We have, among others, an engineer, doctor, government worker, taxi driver, school teacher, and business owner in my neighborhood. Several of my neighbors have interesting talents. There's a drummer nearby who makes lots of noise, an amateur painter who tries to ensnare anyone to sit as her model, a freelance writer, and one man who almost became a professional boxer.

Excelling as a practitioner, and having the ability to instruct others, are different skills.

And me? Like I said, I do kung-fu. I try to do it perfectly, and I'm willing to share it with others.

Though my heartfelt desire is to see kung-fu flourish in the United States and other countries, it is inevitable that I will disappoint many people. To those individuals with their heads full of fantasy and misdirected expectations, I can only say "Sorry, you not only ask of me something I feel is wrong to expect, but I don't even have it."

I do not blame people for asking because they are only repeating the misinformation about kung-fu that persists not only in the United States but the world over. Kung-fu faces a critical problem: Its very survival is at stake because of a terrible shortage of qualified instructors. I feel sorry for those individuals whose unrealistic hopes are dashed when faced with the truth. But I'm even more sorry that real kung-fu can't be enjoyed by more people around the world. My goal is to train qualified instructors in hopes of diminishing the misunderstanding about kung-fu.

Teaching is an art, and not all good practitioners qualify as good teachers. In fact, a practitioner may reach the highest level in his or her style and still fall far short of succeeding as a teacher. Excelling as a practitioner, and having the ability to instruct others, are different skills.

Many practitioners haven't given sufficient thought to what constitutes a qualified teacher. My experience has been that very few students ask how to be a teacher, or even if it is possible for them to become one. Usually, they practice hard and desire to do well or become the best. There is nothing wrong with this. I hope all students strive to reach their potential, but this alone will not qualify one as an instructor.

So what does make a good teacher? I'll break the qualifications into three parts.

First, a teacher needs to be able to provide students with a thorough and correct introduction to the art. Sustaining the interest of students is crucial. It is the rare student who is entirely self-motivated.

Each student is unique, so the instructor must be able to judge each individual's potential and design the training most appropriate to their needs. The train-

The author adjusts a student's arm during his baguazhang workshop in Palo Alto, California.

ing regimen acts as a map, directing the student in a well-defined direction.

One of the initial tasks the instructor faces is to identify and correct the newcomer's bad habits and weaknesses, preparing the student for an eventual full-speed march.

We can see that a qualified teacher is not merely someone who demonstrates a bare-hand or weapons form and expects the student to copy the movement. The teacher who instructs in this manner remains at the level of student, albeit perhaps a senior student. Secondly, a qualified teacher should possess the know-how to design a complete training course for his class or school. A good instructor also needs to be able to create special lessons to help correct the various errors of students.

The traditional training method in China, passed down from generation to generation, is like the Chinese people themselves. Under normal conditions they eat rice, but when they are sick they need the proper herb to keep them alive and help restore their health. I don't mean to equate one's health with kung-fu training, but the kung-fu instructor must take on the responsibility of not only "feeding" the student the correct training, but also must possess the knowledge for "healing" the student whose kung-fu is deficient or impaired.

Basically, a qualified teacher needs a firm grasp of the kung-fu style's elementary material. The best instructors can easily and freely apply what they know to any situation, and can clearly transmit the material to his students. With this as a foundation, a teacher can probably reach the final level, which is to create training methods for the students and pass down authentic kung-fu.

Good instructors are not greedy. They value kung-fu and badly want to share it, rather than covet it like a private heirloom.

This brings us to the attitude requirement, the third key instructor qualification. I've met some people who are 99-percent good kung-fu teachers. Unfortunately, they lack an honest, generous attitude. If instructors lack this quality, they cannot become really good teachers even if they are outstanding in all other ways.

Good instructors are not greedy. They value kung-fu and badly want to share it, rather than covet it like a private heirloom. The success of their students is the greatest reward, and they aspire to have their students surpass them in their skill level. That is the finest and most significant measure of their own success.

The Proper Kung-fu Attitude

The proper development of a person's character and spirit are as important as the physical aspects of kung-fu training. The two elements must be nurtured and grow side by side. Students must first be very patient and willing to commit themselves to a long-range goal. The necessary time must be taken to understand what is gained through the process of learning, rather than dwell only on the intended final product.

I believe it is necessary for students of kung-fu to acknowledge and accept the Chinese tradition and its resulting teacher-student relationship. This relationship is not for the student to judge right or wrong. Students must first take great care in finding a qualified instructor whom they can trust and respect, for it is the teacher who through years of experience and refinement makes available the way (Tao) that the student ultimately seeks.

The traditional relationship doesn't mean that students should blindly devote themselves to the teacher with robot-like obedience.

The traditional relationship doesn't mean that students should blindly devote themselves to the teacher with robot-like obedience. There is a saying in Chinese that can help us to better understand: "The teacher spends three years looking for a student; the student takes three years looking for a teacher."

In ancient times the first part of the saying was more appropriate than today. The teacher had to be very careful to find a student with proper character and ability before teaching him kung-fu. A mistake on the teacher's part in those days could prove dangerous to both himself and to the community.

For today's society, the second part of the saying is more fitting. A capable kung-fu practitioner willing to teach can be hard to find. Often, the teacher will give good students a difficult time, pushing them to the limit (and perhaps beyond), for the purpose of testing both their character and technique.

The teacher should decide not only what the students should learn, but when they should learn it.

The teacher has to see whether they are strong enough and skilled enough to bear the strain. Although the demands may seem unreasonable at the time, students must not withdraw, lose faith, and retreat. Only through trust and perseverance can one's character and spirit grow stronger.

Since coming to the United States to teach, I have often been asked about differences in attitude and ability between Americans and Chinese who study kung-fu. I have found through my teaching experience here that, generally speaking, most American students ask too many questions too soon. An inquisitive mind is not wrong, but too much questioning often signifies that the student failed to practice enough or didn't take enough time to analyze and investigate the problem on his own.

I also have to caution students about being too clever, projecting ahead for movements and technique usage without going through the proper training sequence. Overconfidence can create more harm than good. Just because you can conceive of certain principles and movements (from observing, listening, and imitating) does not automatically mean you can perform them correctly. The teacher should decide not only what the students should learn, but when they should learn it.

Some students believe that respect and admiration are gained by showing off and acting proud. This attitude makes it very difficult for students to learn and improve. They become too easily satisfied with their accomplishments. If they are full, there is no room to grow. One must instead have qualities like bamboo: the higher it grows the more it bends, all the while remaining empty inside.

Kung-fu practitioners should embody what the famous Chinese philosopher Sun Tzu called the Five Morals: Wisdom,

Faithfulness, Humanity, Bravery, and Strictness. Most of all, students who are serious about kung-fu must be honest with themselves, accepting their own shortcomings and limitations and always striving to improve upon them. It requires both strength and courage not only to face the obvious outside enemy, but to admit and face the enemy within.

In daily practice Sun Tzu's principles must be seriously applied in both self-motivation and self-evaluation. Of course, the amount of time spent practicing is important, but what of the quality of the practice? Ask yourself which is better, 10 techniques properly done or 100 techniques performed improperly.

Students who are serious about learning kung-fu must be honest with themselves, accepting their own shortcomings and limitations and always striving to improve upon them.

Each technique should be pushed to the limit, as if your life depended on it. By always demanding improvement and by having a good appctitc for learning, you can remain open-minded enough to continue practicing for a lifetime.

By practicing in the correct way, one can reap the benefits of the kung-fu marital art tradition. And by simultaneously developing character, one trains for direction, focus, and discipline in one's life. Once the mind and personality are cleansed and begin to blossom, it becomes clearly reflected in one's health, appearance, and lifestyle.

Kung-fu's Age of Reason

I am frequently asked to divulge my age. They tend to anticipate one of two answers. I can tell them I am older than my actual
age, and they are impressed by how young I look, attributing my
well-preserved appearance to my kung-fu training. Or I can tell
them I am younger than my age, and that my kung-fu is good
because when I was three years old I was kidnapped by monks
who taught me kung-fu for ten years at their mountain temple. I
might also inform them that I had to kill a bear with my bare hands
and survive a treacherous series of tests to leave the temple.

These stories tend to satisfy preconceived fantasies about
kung-fu. When I was young, I too enjoyed popular legends about
the boy who defeats a large army with his magic sword. I also read
many *Sword Man* fictions and saw
kung-fu movies that depicted very
old men, even partially disabled,
whose kung-fu was extraordinary.
As I grew older, however, I learned
the immortal heroes I read about in
books and saw in movies existed only in the imagination. People
die on the battlefield, and a magic sword cannot prevent someone
with superior skill and physical capabilities from winning the battle.

There are neither 10-year-old instructors, nor 120-year-old masters who can defeat a 25-year-old teacher.

The study of kung-fu, like any other martial art or art form,
cannot impart superhuman powers. There are neither 10-year-old
instructors, nor 120-year-old masters who can defeat a 25-year-old
teacher. Although kung-fu training can slow the aging process, it is
not a fountain of youth.

Some controversy exists about what age is best to start serious kung-fu training. Some teachers believe students should start rigorous training at five to ten years of age. I disagree. Children's bodies are not developed enough to provide a strong foundation and perform the type of hard training required in kung-fu.

Children's bodies undergo a great deal of formative growth during the preteen years. Their tendons, ligaments, muscles, and bones develop substantially during that time. Training that is appropriate for adults may interfere with the natural growth process. The child's body must be more fully developed and balanced before it can be reshaped in a kung-fu way.

Children's training must reflect their special needs and not present an obstacle to their physical or mental development. It should help develop coordination and balance, and give them a basic understanding of kung-fu. When they reach the age where they can begin more rigorous training, they have a rudimentary foundation on which to build.

Among his many fancy toys, the author's childhood favorite was this miniature da dao (giant saber), which he is seen holding in the courtyard of his family home in Nantang, Jiangsu province, China.

Some instructors or parents might say that violence is human nature, and therefore children need the training to defend themselves. There is nothing inherently wrong with that idea, but you need to give children the correct idea about fighting and kung-fu. Children (especially boys) seem to have a natural disposition toward play fighting, which is reinforced by what they see in movies and on television. These misconceptions must be corrected or they will interfere with the learning process.

The appropriate time for children's programs to shift gears into intensive, traditional kung-fu training is junior high school age. Those youngsters who learn from a qualified instructor, receive support from their parents, and train seriously and consistently over an extended period of time have a good chance of becoming accomplished practitioners.

Reaching a high level in kung-fu requires more than the overall physical and technical skill that can be gained from ten years of diligent practice, however. One must acquire an inner understanding and maturity that goes beyond the mere performance of the kung-fu techniques.

The Olympic gymnastic competition provides an illustration of this concept. When I watched the floor exercise competition, I was impressed with the sheer physical power and technical proficiency of the performers. On the other hand, I didn't see much meaning expressed in the forms, only the polished veneer of the techniques. Fundamentally, the majority of gymnasts didn't have the creative

Instructor Mike Veinott is a role model as well as teacher for his young students at the Cupertino Adam Hsu Kung Fu School.

element that invests each movement with meaning, as in poetry. They lack an understanding of what they are doing beyond technique and an ability to give a personal interpretation to the movements. They are performing rather than creating with their art.

The same principle applies to kung-fu. A young practitioner can be proficient, but not capable of being creative in a way that fully captures the spirit of kung-fu. In my experience, I've never seen anyone younger than middle age who can fully show the special creative quality in the kung-fu movements. A high-level kung-fu practitioner can imbue a style with a unique, personal stamp. Even within specific styles of taijiquan, a practitioner can bring a distinctive flavoring to the forms.

As one's kung-fu matures, the changes that occur are often manifest in the way forms are done. If you compare a teacher's form at ages 25, 45, and 65, there will be noticeable differences. Age greatly influences the way one does his forms and affects his kung-fu. Unfortunately, at a time when an instructor's kung-fu is maturing, the effects of aging—the inevitable erosion of physical and mental capabilities—become an obstacle to reaching a higher level. Contrary to some myths about kung-fu, practitioners become physically weaker as they get older.

> *For the student, an older teacher is the best teacher, just as an older, more experienced doctor is generally preferable to one with less experience.*

Some practitioners become disappointed when they realize they cannot reach their intended goal. They may reduce their attention to kung-fu and concentrate on other pursuits. Others continue to pursue their goals as best they can, and some teach kung-fu professionally.

For the student, an older teacher is the best teacher, just as an older, more experienced doctor is generally preferable to one with less experience. During this transition period, however, the teacher's attitude toward the young student may change. Some become bitter and jealous, seeing their students as potential rivals and a threat to their authority. They still have a selfish dream to be the only teacher of their art, and they are afraid their students will surpass their skill. Thus, they may be unwilling to share their knowledge and experience with the deserving student.

A selfish attitude is harmful to the teacher, the student, and kung-fu in general. The only way to overcome the disappointment associated with the realization of our human limits is to pass the treasures we possess onto the next generation to insure that the art doesn't die. Just as parents enjoy the success of their children, teachers should help students reach their potential.

Although the instructor becomes weaker with age, there are some mitigating factors. With a strong kung-fu foundation and good training, an instructor's power and speed will fade more slowly. The most important principle that allows a teacher to show tremendous power and skill beyond middle age is that kung-fu doesn't rely on raw power. Kung-fu techniques rely on *chan si jin* (silk reeling energy) to generate power from the effect of the body's joints, tendons, muscles, and bones working together as a unit.

Hiding from the inevitable physical and mental deterioration is impossible, except in the fantasy world of kung-fu legends and movies. On the other hand, by practicing seriously and establishing a strong kung-fu foundation, taking care of oneself in terms of dietary and daily habits, and not worrying about getting old can help you delay the aging process and maintain your kung-fu skill.

The Senior Student

In recent years, Chinese kung-fu teachers from all over the world have come to the West to share their knowledge. Many of these teachers are products of cultures and training regimens considerably different from those usually found in the United States.

In general, the cultural environment from which kung-fu was born and has blossomed offers a striking contrast to Western ideas of teaching and learning. In China, for example, the purpose of education has always extended beyond acquiring knowledge. The long, difficult, and rigorous hours spent at school or with tutors were intended to develop not only intellectual skills but, more importantly, foster the cultivation and refinement of character and personality.

By setting a good example both physically and in attitude, the senior students serve as a cultural bridge between the junior students and the Chinese instructor.

Largely due to the pervasive influence of Confucianism, oral principles and teachings have been tightly woven into the very fabric of Chinese life. Traditionally in China, the teacher is held in a highly respected and revered position. Students obey the teacher's instructions dutifully and without question. The discipline and obedience provides students with the secure foundation necessary for leading a successful and harmonious life. Only after a skill has been mastered through precise and repeated practice will creativity and originality emerge. This outlook and approach is dramatically different from what most Westerners have experienced. Americans are less willing to accept the "just do it and one day you'll understand" answer and as a whole desire more feedback.

Some instructors are able to adapt their kung-fu to fit the American character, but many understandably find it difficult or even impossible to change their approach. In some instances, instructors who become less Americanized can be popular and successful. The pidgin-speaking teacher clad in traditional Chinese dress more closely fits the American image and ideal of a real kung-fu master. Learning in a Chinese environment with such a teacher not only serves to attract many students to study, but it is thought by many to indicate the high quality of an instructor's kung-fu.

> Where the instructor may only explain and demonstrate the techniques a few times, the senior student is available for repeated explanations and demonstrations

Regardless of learning preference, it is clear that problems and misunderstandings arise when the Chinese teacher presents an art as traditional and complex as kung-fu to a Western public.

Making the transition from East to West has been helped greatly by the presence of American senior students. They are familiar with the instructor's personality and teaching style, and understand the unique problems that Americans face in learning kung-fu.

By setting a good example both physically and in attitude, the senior students serve as a cultural bridge between the junior students and the Chinese instructor. Without a cultural barrier between junior and senior, the latter can more readily provide the necessary support and encouragement many of the newer students require.

Junior students can look to the senior to gain more insight into the overall nature of the art itself as well as to receive feedback on their training. Where the instructor may only explain and demonstrate the techniques a few times, the senior student is available for repeated explanations and demonstrations. Senior students can also help minimize any misconceptions or misunderstandings, helping fellow students improve and mature both technically and emotionally.

By practicing diligently and behaving conscientiously—not just for their own personal growth and satisfaction or to please their teachers—senior students can provide an all important intermediate model for the junior and beginning students.

Because of valuable experience and insights gained from their responsibilities and position, senior students often become assistant instructors and play an even more active role in the class. Many go on to open kung-fu schools of their own.

Yet care must be taken to avoid the pitfalls that can often accompany these responsibilities. Senior students can potentially discredit not only themselves but also their teachers. A common problem is senior students who attempt to imitate the instructor as closely as possible. They not only emulate their teacher's kung-fu, but also the style of dress, mannerisms, and sometimes even likes and dislikes. Such senior students become a carbon copy imitation and in many cases may be even stricter and more severe than their teachers.

In order to encourage and assist younger, promising, or superior-talented students, senior students must respect kung-fu by being honest and open-minded when it comes to working with their juniors. Mistreatment, discouragement, and holding back information because of jealousy defeats the whole ideal of the senior student's position and, more importantly, the purpose of his kung-fu training.

Rather than fall prey to these shortcomings, senior students should try to realize their responsibilities and develop their own teaching skills within the framework of the art. By striving unceasingly to realize and strengthen their weak points and perfect their skills, senior students can effectively promote not only their teachers but the entire art of kung-fu as well.

Belt Levels for Kung-fu?

The place is north China. The time, a foregone era. The warning: "Be careful brother, here comes a black belt and the shuaijiao (Chinese wrestling) black belt does not come to play."

The black belt has always been regarded as a high rank, but if we go back in time, we find the black belt was not always black. Long ago, serious practitioners of shuaijiao had a saying: "Once you put on the *da lian,* be prepared to die." The *da lian* (a special, tight-fitting jacket still worn by shuaijiao practitioners) is a short-sleeved garment without ties, buttons, or zippers to close the front. It is made of a durable fabric (usually hemp or camel hair) and comes in either light brown or white. The belt used to hold the jacket closed is also made of hemp.

When a shuaijiao practitioner put on the *da lian,* he was responsible for his destiny. Shuaijiao matches are usually held in a sand pit, where the combination of sweat and dirt stains the *da lian.* While the wrestler will clean his *da lian,* the belt is not usually washed. Through prolonged use, the once white belt turns black. The condition or color of an opponent's belt determines the level of his skill.

I want to encourage my kung-fu teachers to develop a system of level classification, similar to the belt system, to promote the art.

Around the end of the 19th-century in Japan, Jigoro Kano created judo, emphasizing its moral and educational aspects rather than brutal techniques. One of Kano's greatest innovations was classifying judo's different degrees: the five stages leading to the level of black belt. Unlike the

A Han dynasty stone rubbing of the ancestor of shuaijiao. When a shuaijiao practitioner put on the da lian, he was responsible for his destiny

shuaijiao black belt, the judo belt comes in black and is made of cotton.

Judo has different levels of black belt as well as higher degrees represented by different colored belts. The qualifications for the different colored belts are not determined by testing the practitioner's technique, but rather are based upon the student's dedication to judo. A committee studies the practitioner's promotion and teaching of the art, published writings, educational level, manner, and position in society.

Kano could be called a true pioneer because he adapted judo to the changing times and devised methods of determining the practitioner's level. Private death matches, once used to determine rank, were no longer tolerated. Belonging to the judo community means having a clear understanding of its hierarchy. The system is intelligent and well structured, minimizing the chance of internal conflict. Tolerating disrespectful behavior of any kind conveys an unfavorable image, making the sport unattractive to the outsider.

Other martial arts—Japanese karate and Korean taekwondo, for example—have borrowed from judo's orderly system to promote their respective styles.

I would like to see kung-fu develop a similar system. The absence of a ranking system in traditional kung-fu blurs the picture in terms of clear-cut levels, standards and expectations that go along with them. As a result, many students feel unsure of their abilities and goals, and frequently become discouraged.

Creating a ranking system certainly would be difficult, but not impossible, if the psychological barrier can be overcome. The Chinese, especially kung-fu teachers, resist applying elements of Japanese origin. Learning from the Japanese, however, would not constitute a great break from tradition. Since the end of the Qing dynasty (1911), the Chinese have studied the Japanese systems of science, technology, military strategy, law, and economics.

There is no shame in learning. I want to encourage my kung-fu teachers to develop a system of level classification, similar to the belt system, to promote the art. Kung-fu has different styles that need standards for belts, such as form performance, sparring, and power testing.

With any new venture, a period of trial and error is expected. Don't be discouraged right away if everything fails to go according to plan. Instead, teachers and students should embrace the opportunity to breathe new life into this ancient martial art. Test the different ideas until you develop a system with which you feel comfortable. The testing of each style should be separate, while standards for basic training, sparring, and form performance that spotlight the flavor of the art should be established. Weapons training should also be standardized.

The testing of each style should be separate, while standards for basic training, sparring, and form performance that spotlight the flavor of the art should be established.

In time, we can establish standards in broader categories, such as northern and southern styles. Perhaps unified standards can be established for all kung-fu styles.

When kung-fu was a tool of survival, secrecy and deception were its foundations. But kung-fu's essence has always been its ability to change. Despite the obvious difficulties lying ahead, I am excited about kung-fu's future. In order for the art to survive, it must remain adaptable. An appropriate banner for its march into the future would be the dirty belt that gradually turns black.

Salute! I'm Your Grandpa

When I first arrived in San Francisco in the late 1970s I was really surprised and impressed by the high level of Chinese kung-fu. There were so many different styles, respected schools, and famous teachers. Literally, it was the kung-fu capital of the world outside of China. I organized several major performances and helped my kung-fu friends produce very successful demonstrations as well. As we expected, the high level techniques displayed were superb. Predictably, the audience's response was great. There were no problems, nothing unforeseen, with one surprising exception.

I was really shocked when some teachers protested, argued, and complained about their titles. I had respectfully called everybody *"Sifu."* It is the Chinese word for "teacher," and is used in any business or field. It never occurred to me that any of the teachers

Sifu Tu Yi Che was my Chen taiji-quan sifu, and should be called shiye by my taiji students.

would be dissatisfied and disappointed with the title. Later on I found out that some *sifus* preferred to be called "master," which they felt was a higher level than *sifu.* I dashed to check my dictionary and found that if *sifu* equals teacher than master is truly higher than teacher. But now came another question: Who qualified those teachers as masters or even grandmasters?

So far there is no authority commonly recognized within kung-fu's population for setting standards, providing exams, and judging any kung-fu practitioner's level of technique. And sadly, the kung-fu community isn't powerful enough to be a voice that commands the attention of politicians and governments, whether national, state, county, or city level.

Let's check the facts. Acupuncturists, at least in some states, must take classes, pass examinations, and comply with continuous education requirements to earn and maintain their licenses to practice. For kung-fu and qigong, no requirements exist for anyone who wishes to teach or open a school.

The lack of a controlling authority, standardized qualifications, and examination requirements certainly has produced a big leak. Some people are simply brave enough to crown themselves "master." On the other hand, many great kung-fu masters not only have very high-level technique but also the highest morals. They are forever humble and possess both tireless teaching and learning attitudes. In my judgment, I believe those are the real masters. However they don't even feel comfortable accepting the title *"sifu"* or "master." They prefer to call themselves practitioners, martial arts lovers, eternal wushu students, and so forth.

> *For kung-fu and qigong, no requirements exist for anyone who wishes to teach or open a school.*

As you can see, the real masters are not officially using their titles, whereas many less qualified masters can use the title as they wish without any control or limitation. Nowadays in martial arts circles, the term *sifu* is a reliable title. To clarify this, think back to grammar school: we learn that some teachers are good and some lousy. Likewise in kung-fu, a *sifu* can be good or bad. "Master" is really not a reliable title. Once people hear the title "master," a question mark, not respect, appears in their minds.

Some people call themselves *shiye* or *shigong.* In Chinese, *ye* and *gong* mean "grandpa." Even though the person isn't really a family grandparent but related through the teacher-student association, we call our teacher's father *shiye* or *shigong.* Only in one's own system will the disciple call the master's father or teacher *shiye* or *shigong*. Like sifu, these naming conventions also apply to other fields besides kung-fu.

The various titles have been misused over the centuries, however. Using *shiye* and *shigong* inappropriately came from some martial artists who ignored cultural propriety to entertain their own personal egos. This was one method they used in trying to establish authority.

I have also seen several of my martial arts colleagues who teach club sports that are not even part of the regular curriculum in college call themselves "professor." Some are even officially using "grand-professor," a title not to be found on the rosters of public universities.

I personally do not know where that came from. "Professor" is a professional title used in our society. There are required standards to pass before being qualified for that title. If the martial arts

community wishes to establish its own professional titles I do agree we could use terms that already exist in our society such as coach, instructor, and professor, or respect kung-fu's cultural background and use the terms coming from its country of origin.

Much more important than terms and titles, we should set up a ranking system to control quality.

Sifu Liu Yun Chiao, in his seventies, performs the kun wu sword form during his 1982 trip to the United States.

Then when a person reaches a certain level, whatever title he has is inconsequential for he has earned respect.

Am I a grandpa yet? Yes. As a matter of fact, I'm even a great-grandpa in martial arts. Several years ago, Chinese wrestling *sifu* and professor, Chang Guan Ming, led his team from the Kao Shung Technological College to tour the United States and met with me and other *sifus* in San Francisco. He introduced the San Francisco contingent to his team members as *sifu*. He pointed to me, however, and told his students "This is your *shiye*," because Professor Chang Guan Ming was my student in the physical education department of Taiwan Normal University. So his pupils called me *shiye* to show their respect within our own family tree. Though they addressed the other great, local teachers as *sifu*, it didn't reduce their respect for them. Although some of these *sifus* are older than me and their achievements in kung-fu are obviously higher than mine, still they should not be called *shiye* or *shigong*.

> The real masters are not officially using their titles, whereas many less qualified masters can use the title as they wish without any control or limitation.

So, I am a great-grandpa because many of my students' students are now teaching. However, by any account this is just in my family and not your business. So practitioners who are not in my family should not call me Grandpa Hsu but just Sifu Hsu because I'm a kung-fu teacher, or Mr. Hsu because you are an educated person.

Part 8

Kung-fu
Today and Tomorrow

The Complete Kung-fu Practitioner

When I started to teach kung-fu in San Francisco about 20 years ago, I was surprised, and sometimes a little frightened, by some of the questions students asked me. In China, no matter where you teach kung-fu—at a university, kung-fu studio, or in private—prospective students only want to verify your kung-fu abilities.

A kung-fu practitioner who studies any other disciplines in Chinese culture will gain a greater understanding of the yin and yang principle.

In the United States, students ask me: Do you know acupuncture? What do you know about herbs? What classical Chinese instrument do you play? Have you had opera training? When my answers are not satisfactory, some of these students then want to know if I am a philosopher.

Many people in the San Francisco area are interested in Asian culture. As a Chinese person, I'm glad to see that Westerners want to learn about Asian cultures. However, it's difficult for me to see any direct relationship between various areas of Chinese culture and kung-fu.

Kung-fu is a product of Chinese culture. If you have some grasp of Chinese philosophy, art, literature, or music, it can help your kung-fu. But don't think that any of these arts can take the place of kung-fu practice. Let's be clear about the real relationship among Chinese arts. If you want to study Chinese medicine, I can recommend an excellent Chinese doctor, but this doctor cannot demonstrate kung-fu, sing Chinese opera, or write classical poetry. If your major interest is Chinese painting, I know several good

Chinese painters, but none of them can perform acupuncture, teach Chinese folk dancing, or play any Chinese instruments.

The points I'm making are simple. First, very few kung-fu teachers are experts in other arts. I am not, and I don't wish to cultivate other arts because my primary art is kung-fu. If my kung-fu is excellent, that is enough for me.

Remember that the East and the West are separated by the Pacific Ocean, both physically and culturally. For several hundred years people have migrated to the West from the East. The East has learned much from Western civilization in the areas of science, democracy, art, and philosophy. Conversely, Westerners who seek Eastern wisdom must understand that it is impossible to include all aspects of Asian culture under one discipline. The Westerner who wants to complete a voyage to the East, not only to reach the shores but to discover the interior Eastern culture, must realize that such a trip can only be made step by step. It requires a humble attitude, patience, and perseverance.

Since most of my students are Westerners, I ask them to learn as much as possible about Chinese culture. This can help their kung-fu, and it can make my job of teaching much easier. This extracurricular study doesn't mean my students can replace their kung-fu practice with a visit to a Chinese restaurant. On the contrary, the only way to learn kung-fu is to practice kung-fu.

Stilt-walkers in colorful costumes perform this traditional acrobatic Chinese folk art.

Naturally, I agree that Chinese medicine, such as acupuncture, herbs, and physical therapy, is closely related to kung-fu. If we understand our bodies, it's easier to practice our martial art. Kung-fu involves many vigorous movements, low stances, applications, and sparring sessions. Over the years, it's difficult to avoid injury. If you are injured, however, a knowledge of acupuncture and herbs can really help. These kinds of medical skills are a marvelous supplement to kung-fu, but again, they are only supplements, not substitutes.

Don't hide weaknesses in your training behind a superficial knowledge of other Chinese cultural disciplines.

Another way students can gain more knowledge of Chinese culture is to learn more about the theory of *yin* and *yang*. This theory permeates Chinese culture. A kung-fu practitioner who studies any other disciplines in Chinese culture will gain a greater understanding of the *yin* and *yang* principle.

Accordingly, the principle of *yin* and *yang* applies to kung-fu. Many kung-fu styles, such as taijiquan, use the *yin/yang* symbol as a trademark of their system. Furthermore, all kung-fu styles use this principle to explain their theory and techniques, but even a deep knowledge of the *yin/yang* principle will only give you a key to open the outer gate to the palace of kung-fu. When you step inside that palace, you will still only be on the threshold. To go past the gate and into the inner realms of the palace, you must practice your kung-fu. Nothing can substitute for serious practice.

If kung-fu is the Chinese cultural expression you choose, make it your priority. Practice seriously, correctly, and patiently. Use your brain, not just your body. Above all, don't hide weaknesses in your training behind a superficial knowledge of other Chinese cultural disciplines. Martial arts must be based on honesty. Don't lie to yourself. Don't pretend that your kung-fu is powerful because you know some Chinese philosophy; you could get killed that way. To defend yourself against an assailant, you must know blocks, kicks, and punches. You can't stop an attacker by quoting Confucius. Remember, if you cheat, you only cheat yourself.

The True Lessons of Fighting

In the martial arts, we learn to fight. We are trained to protect ourselves and our loved ones. Kung-fu is no different, although this is not the final purpose of the art. Developing into a good fighter should not be the incentive for studying any martial art. Why, then, should you learn kung-fu if you are not going to use it? Why practice for endless hours filled with pain and self-denial to master techniques that will never be tested?

Obviously, knowing how to defend yourself is still necessary under certain circumstances. On the streets, it is often a case of kill or be killed, so martial arts training must be difficult and demanding. Unfortunately, even with untiring dedication to training, not everyone can become a good fighter. There are no guarantees.

The martial arts also provide an excellent form of holistic exercise, fully balanced and in harmony with the body's basic principles. Herein lies the true benefit of learning a martial art. The student is provided with a unique form of moral and character development that is difficult—if not impossible—to acquire from school, family, religious institutions, or any other aspect of society.

A Confucian saying states: "If you can't be honest, nothing can happen."

In the martial arts, the body is used as a vehicle for personal realization and development. From the beginning, systematic kung-fu training teaches the student to endure the painful rigors of recasting his body into the kung-fu mold. As the body changes and develops, so does the mind and character. The practitioner begins to internalize and actualize what previously were only empty intellectual concepts, like patience, perseverance, mental resoluteness, physical diligence and toil, faith, trust, and confidence in himself and the teacher.

From the beginning, systematic kung-fu training teaches the student to endure the painful rigors of recasting his body into the kung-fu mold.

During the next stage of practice, students focus all their energy into a specific style. By absorbing his style's unique flavor, techniques and specialties, they continue to develop and improve their character and personality. The kung-fu student realizes precision, self-control, physical and mental balance, creativity, and beauty. The movements begin to reflect the student's state of mind, and the student's state of mind reflects the movements.

When training for real usage, the student analyzes step-by-step the techniques learned from the forms. There are two-person forms, and eventually free sparring, where the harsh reality of fighting becomes shockingly and painfully evident. Perhaps you strike a classmate by mistake and feel regret, or get injured because you can't effectively protect yourself yet. Everyone must go through these steps in order to become a good martial artist. From the reality of combat, the practitioner can reach even deeper inside, touching qualities such as truth and honesty, facing themselves and the enemy as well. These qualities are manifested in students and become an integrated part of their lives.

A Confucian saying states: "If you can't be honest, nothing can happen." And in Zen Buddhism, the statement "Purify your heart and see your real nature" also serves to remind us of ideals we must keep in mind throughout our lives.

But how do we transfer this knowledge to our daily affairs when we live in a society that takes people and categorizes, compartmentalizes, and files them, tossing them aside and ignoring them? We have come to judge ourselves, our value as human beings, by our successes, failures, and all the artificial standards created for us by society. That person is a millionaire, the woman on his arm is a beauty queen, and that young guy over there has three Ph.Ds. Being able to easily and conveniently attach a label to people and situations doesn't mean you have an understanding of them.

Who are you really? Do you honestly know yourself, or are you a mass produced by-product of Madison Avenue? Have you ever been truly tested in this world of superficial values and intellectual symbolism?

In the martial arts, the body is used as a vehicle for personal realization and development.

Martial arts is the great equalizer. In fighting situations, everyone stands on their own. Your Mercedes, high-priced lawyers, and credit cards can't buy your safety. Rich or poor, handsome or ugly, when a punch is thrown in your direction you'll either block it or get knocked down. You choose.

Whether you are an excellent or poor fighter isn't the point. We use fighting as a tool to slice away the layers of illusion, to uncover and acquaint each of us with our true selves. This is the real training. These are invaluable and irreplaceable lessons we learn from kung-fu.

Pursuing the Ultimate Kung-fu Goals

I have spent most of my adult lifetime studying and research-ing kung-fu, and have learned many lessons. One of the major lessons brings me all the way back to the beginning days of my training. It may seem obvious, but I must say emphatically that the practice of martial arts should not be for others but for the practi-tioners themselves.

Most young people who learn kung-fu are willing to sweat, expend great amounts of energy, and undertake this hardship all for a useless goal: to impress others. It can be as simple as impressing one's parents, amusing a girlfriend, or showing off in front of the kids at school.

Good kung-fu comes about when you concentrate on making yourself good rather than on how to hurt others.

They strike the bag and kick the post to turn their human body made of flesh and blood into a piece of iron. They're willing to pay the highest price to purchase the top secret death touch or enroll in supernatural *qi* training. They throw themselves into unreal, unnecessary, and unhealthy training, trading their well being for short-term glory.

My purpose in bringing up this issue is not to toss critical darts at my fellow kung-fu practitioners but to admit that I regret-fully have done some of these stupid things. I have focused on the other person and on inflicting damage. Good kung-fu comes about when you concentrate on making yourself good rather than on how to hurt others. Clearly, in our modern society techniques that heal are far more valuable than those that maim or kill.

To reach kung-fu's highest levels and earn its rewards, we know how important it is to practice hard. Youth and strength don't automatically bestow real potential in kung-fu training. We arrive in this world as humans and undergo a lengthy education from family, school, and society to become civilized humans. Kung-fu training is similar: Everyone is born with a different natural physical makeup, and those who have stronger muscles, bigger bones, superior nerve pathways, and healthier organs are said to have athletic ability.

Kung-fu's fundamental requirements exceed the boundaries of the natural. Effective kung-fu training must bother, challenge, pressure, and develop the practitioner's mental muscle. The practitioner will then have the ability to develop the *qi* to utilize with the body, coordinating the internal and external to work together. In this way, kung-fu training does change one's philosophy, and the world is viewed in a different manner.

If we are required to confront the battlefield in our daily lives, whether on the national or neighborhood level, it will be necessary to focus our attention on our enemies. We must acquire certain skills and apply them to get the job done. Under these circumstances, we are not talking about martial arts. From a purely martial arts standpoint, we sacrifice a great deal from training focused

The author leads his coaches in doing internal training in the "kung-fu garden" of his Cupertino, California home.

on external forces. In fact, it becomes a total sacrifice. We give up the possibility to be good in martial arts, but at least we have fulfilled our duty to serve and complete the mission. When weighed against soldiers sacrificing their lives on the battlefield, just sacrificing the chance to excel in martial arts is not such a big deal.

When I was a little boy, like all Chinese, I learned that selfishness is the fountain of sin, crime, and degradation. We children worked hard to erase all selfishness from our hearts, even though it is part of our human nature. Selflessness and generosity are the good and necessary foundation of a happy, peaceful, harmonious society.

When I entered high school and started my serious kung-fu training, the government required all students to study Confucianism. We had to read and memorize the "Four Books."

One day I was shocked to read, "In ancient times, students studied for themselves. Nowadays, students study for others."

"Ancient times," to Confucius, were the "good old days" where people lived correctly and did the right thing. "Nowadays," on the other hand, was Confucius's own time, which he always criticized as a miserable era in which people did many things wrong. On first glance, this statement appeared to be 180-degrees incorrect. Surely, to study for yourself was the epitome of selfishness, whereas those who studied for others put society's needs first.

The author's father holding a hook sword.

Of course, I was wrong and my teacher set the record straight: Confucius tried to point out that in the old days, people studied hard in order to understand the meaning of life, develop high moral standards within themselves, and cultivate correct attitudes toward each other. They studied to improve themselves so that they could contribute the best possible service to their society.

Around the time Confucius lived, the government was starting to select educated people to work for the ruling dynasty in high positions. The education of that era took a self-centered turn. People

Kung-fu training can be likened to a straight highway that links beginner to master.

studied in order to impress and amuse the lords of the kingdom. They polished their movements, language, clothing, and social manners so that they could climb into higher social strata and gather as much authority and power.

Although the products of this education might develop useful skills and marketable abilities, their basic orientation had become the benefit of the self or group to which they might have allegiance. They were lacking in moral controls, and ignored the needs of the majority. This damaged society and gave rise to great problems.

Later on when I taught classical Chinese literature in the university, I liked to tell my students this story. I wanted to give them a real example of how dangerous a misinterpretation could be. More significant than specific class materials, it was important that they learn a lesson from my own experience so that they would approach the study of any ancient Chinese art with the correct awareness and attitude.

I hope this story is also interesting and inspiring to those for whom kung-fu training is important. I believe the majority of young people who practice kung-fu for others don't have selfish motivations. They need to be shown the way, but unfortunately the true meaning of kung-fu is almost never openly promoted and taught to kung-fu students.

How your training begins is extraordinarily important. Kung-fu training can be likened to a straight highway that links beginner to master. If your first, basic step diverges one degree, one-half, or even one-quarter from the true direction, then after weeks, months, years, or even decades of practice, the most dedicated practitioner can end up a monumental distance from his or her cherished goal.

Today many kung-fu practitioners have no idea they are on the wrong track. Happily and innocently, they are contributing the extinction of kung-fu. Another group of practitioners has at some point discovered their error. They are disappointed, frustrated, and angry, which leads them to stop their training. A small minority realize their mistake after it's too late to turn their heads back. They are unwilling to face the truth, so they keep promoting kung-fu the old way, misleading their followers, enlarging the scope of the mistake and hastening the arrival of kung-fu's death.

Confucius is long gone but Confucianism is still alive. It has even survived brutal attacks by the Chinese communists, especially during the Cultural Revolution. Today the philosophy is studied and appreciated by three different groups. The first is made up of schools that understand, preserve, and promote Confucius' ideas, and modernize them to fit into our society. The second group knows about Confucius, is familiar with his work, but doesn't really comprehend his works. The third group totally misunderstands him. Kung-fu has a parallel situation. The second group is the majority. They practice kung-fu but cannot touch its essence. The third group we can ignore because no matter what we say or do, it will exist.

We must focus our attention, with all honesty, on taking whatever steps are necessary to raise ourselves and as many other practitioners as possible into the first group: real kung-fu artists of high level who pass our inheritance on to future generations.

About the Author

Sifu Adam Hsu was born in Shanghai, China and emigrated to Taiwan where he spent twenty-five years studying with the most respected kung-fu masters. His first teacher was Sifu Han Ching Tan. His principle teacher was the late Grandmaster Liu Yun Chiao.

He has a master's degree in Chinese literature and has taught this subject at Taiwan Normal University. He is the former editor and publisher of *Wu Tang Martial Arts Magazine* and a past senior editor of the Kung-fu Library of Wu Chow Publishing Company, the largest publisher of kung-fu literature. He has had several books published in Chinese, and over a hundred articles printed throughout the world in English, Chinese, Japanese, German, Italian, Spanish, and Russian.

In 1978, Sifu Hsu moved to the United States where he has been teaching traditional northern style kung-fu in the San Francisco Bay Area. The curriculum at his schools includes Chen taijiquan, baguazhang, changquan, bajiquan, and authentic, traditional kung-fu bare-hand and weapons sparring.

In 1990 he founded the Traditional Wushu Association, a non-profit corporation dedicated to the preservation, promotion, and modernization of traditional kung-fu. The Association has successfully introduced and promoted traditional kung-fu weapons free-sparring as an activity for tournament competition. Its most recent project is the creation and development of ranking systems for traditional kung-fu styles. The association also offers a service that connects students who wish to study in China with the real traditional masters.

Adam Hsu Kung Fu School
PO Box 1075
Cupertino, CA 95015-1075
phone/fax: (650) 326-8253
http://www-leland.stanford.edu/~sunspark/kungfu/